Brodie

Also From Aurora Rose Reynolds

The Until Series
Until November
Until Trevor
Until Lilly
Until Nico
Second Chance Holiday

Until Her Series
Until July
Until June
Until Ashlyn
Until Harmony
Until December
Until April
Until May
Until Willow
Until Hanna

Until Him Series
Until Jax
Until Sage
Until Cobi
Until Talon

Shooting Stars Series
Fighting to Breathe
Wide-Open Spaces
One Last Wish

Underground Kings Series
Assumption
Obligation
Distraction
Infatuation

Ruby Falls Series
Falling Fast

One More Time

Fluke My Life Series
Running into Love
Stumbling into Love
Tossed into Love
Drawn into Love

Before Series
Before We Fall
Before This Ends

How to Catch an Alpha Series
Catching Him
Baiting Him
Hooking Him

Adventures In Love Series
Rushed
Risky
Reckless

1001 Dark Nights
Keeping You
Brodie

Stand-Alone Novels
Love at the Bluebird
The Wrong/Right Man
For nEver
Alpha Law (written as C. A. Rose)
Justified (written as C. A. Rose)
Liability (written as C. A. Rose)
Finders Keepers (written as C. A. Rose)

To Have to Hold to Keep Series
Trapping Her

Brodie
An Until Her Novella
By Aurora Rose Reynolds

1001 DARK NIGHTS
PRESS

Brodie
An Until Her Novella
By Aurora Rose Reynolds

1001 Dark Nights

Copyright 2024 Aurora Rose Reynolds
ISBN: 979-8-88542-067-9

Foreword: Copyright 2014 M. J. Rose

Published by 1001 Dark Nights Press, an imprint of Evil Eye Concepts, Incorporated

All rights reserved. No part of this book may be reproduced, scanned, or distributed in any printed or electronic form without permission. Please do not participate in or encourage piracy of copyrighted materials in violation of the author's rights.

This is a work of fiction. Names, places, characters and incidents are the product of the author's imagination and are fictitious. Any resemblance to actual persons, living or dead, events or establishments is solely coincidental.

Acknowledgments from the Author

THANK YOU. I never feel like those two words are enough to express how grateful I am when a reader takes a chance on one of my stories, but those words are all I have, so they'll have to do. Without each of you this dream of mine would not be a possibility so I hope you know how much I appreciate you.

Thank you, bloggers and book pushers, for your unwavering dedication to reading and spreading that joy.

Thank you to my family and friends who are always cheering me on, especially my two guys.

Extra big thanks to Liz Berry, Jillian Stein, and Melisse Rose. Thank you for allowing me to write for 1001 Dark Nights. It's always such a fun experience. I appreciate you and the entire 1001 Dark Nights/Blue Box Press team.

One Thousand and One Dark Nights

Once upon a time, in the future...

I was a student fascinated with stories and learning. I studied philosophy, poetry, history, the occult, and the art and science of love and magic. I had a vast library at my father's home and collected thousands of volumes of fantastic tales.

I learned all about ancient races and bygone times. About myths and legends and dreams of all people through the millennium. And the more I read the stronger my imagination grew until I discovered that I was able to travel into the stories... to actually become part of them.

I wish I could say that I listened to my teacher and respected my gift, as I ought to have. If I had, I would not be telling you this tale now. But I was foolhardy and confused, showing off with bravery.

One afternoon, curious about the myth of the Arabian Nights, I traveled back to ancient Persia to see for myself if it was true that every day Shahryar (Persian: شهريار, "king") married a new virgin, and then sent yesterday's wife to be beheaded. It was written and I had read that by the time he met Scheherazade, the vizier's daughter, he'd killed one thousand women.

Something went wrong with my efforts. I arrived in the midst of the story and somehow exchanged places with Scheherazade – a phenomena that had never occurred before and that still to this day, I cannot explain.

Now I am trapped in that ancient past. I have taken on Scheherazade's life and the only way I can protect myself and stay alive is to do what she did to protect herself and stay alive.

Every night the King calls for me and listens as I spin tales. And when the evening ends and dawn breaks, I stop at a point that leaves him breathless and yearning for more. And so the King spares my life for one more day, so that he might hear the rest of my dark tale.

As soon as I finish a story... I begin a new one... like the one that you, dear reader, have before you now.

Prologue

Reese

I don't know exactly what wakes me up, but when my cell on the nightstand beeps, I reach over and pick up my glasses, putting them on before grabbing my phone and bringing it close to my face so I can read the screen. Frowning at the notification informing me that Kirk finished a workout, I realize that I picked up *his* phone attached to his watch, which keeps track of his steps and how many calories he's burned in a day. I glance behind me and find him gone. The two of us were up late studying for a test last night, so he stayed over rather than drive back to his apartment near our campus. It's something he does on occasion when Richard and my mom are out of town like they are now.

Richard, my mom's fiancé, travels a lot for work and likes Mom to go with him, leaving me alone in the house for days at a time—unless Richard's daughter, Melissa, decides to stay here rather than on campus with her sorority. Which rarely happens.

I look at the time in the corner of the phone. It's a little after two in the morning—an odd time to work out—but Kirk has been stressed about the test he has coming up. Maybe he needed to burn off some energy.

Sitting up, I toss back the covers and get out of bed to check on him. After I drag a hoodie over my sleep tank and shove my feet into my slippers, I leave my bedroom on the second floor, Kirk's phone in hand. The house is dark and quiet, and, if I'm honest…a little creepy, which is why I often ask Kirk to stay over. I hate being here alone.

Hearing a bump as I start down the stairs, a sense of unease slithers through my insides.

I'm about to turn, head up the stairs, and go back to my room, but I freeze in the stairway when I hear a door open and then a familiar giggle.

My heart pounding, I peek around the corner and watch Melissa, wrapped in the robe I got her for Christmas, kiss Kirk in a way I *never* have.

Pressing my hand against my stomach, I slowly back up one step and freeze again when the stair creaks under my weight.

"What was that?" I hear Melissa whisper, my heart pounding in panic.

I turn to rush up the stairs, but my slippers slide on the shiny wood, causing me to fall as I fumble for the railing. My glasses slide off my face as I skid down the steps, my footwear doing nothing to keep me on my feet. I land on my ass.

"Reese?" Melissa says in disbelief. I squint, unable to really see her.

"Shit, Reese, are you okay?" Kirk gasps, rushing up the steps to my side.

"I'm fine." I shake him off when he grabs my arm to help me up.

"What are you doing out here?" My fingers make contact with my glasses, and I put them on. *What am I doing out here?* Gritting my teeth, I stand. My bottom is so sore I know I'll have more than just the bruise to my ego tomorrow.

"How long?" I look between the two of them while desperately trying to ignore the pain in my throat.

"Reese." Kirk takes a step toward me, guilt written all over his handsome face. I look at Melissa. She doesn't look guilty; she appears almost…victorious? I shouldn't be surprised; she hates me, and I'm sure she feels like she just won some battle I didn't even know I was in.

"How long?" I repeat.

"It just happened," Kirk says quietly.

"So, tonight?" I look between them again, knowing in one glance that it's happened before.

"Reese." Kirk takes another step toward me.

Holding up my hand, I back up and then toss him the phone I somehow never dropped, turning on my slippers to head up the stairs—thankfully, staying on my feet.

"Reese," Kirk calls, following me. "I'm sorry." *Sorry?* Yeah, right. I'm sure he's only sorry he got caught. "Please, just talk to me," he pleads.

"No." I shake my head.

"It just happened; I didn't mean for it to happen."

"So, what? You just accidentally slept with her?" When I reach my door, I turn to glare at him.

"I just..." He drags his fingers through his long hair. "I just..."

"Come on, Kirk. Leave her alone," Melissa calls. I look over at her. I don't know why she hates me. I've never understood what I did to deserve it. I'm not competition. My mom loves her, maybe even more than she loves me. She's the kind of daughter Mom always wanted, and they get along like best friends. I'm the outsider, the awkward one.

"It doesn't matter." I grab the door handle with a shaking hand.

"I know it *does* matter," Kirk whispers, and I turn my head to look at him.

"You're right." I feel a single stupid tear trailing down my cheek. "It does matter because you're supposed to be my best friend." I turn the handle, push the door in only enough to get inside, then shut it behind me and lock it.

"Reese." Kirk pounds on the wood.

Ignoring him, I kick off my slippers and crawl into bed, trying to wrap my head around what just happened and how I feel about it.

I've known Kirk since we were four, and we have been best friends ever since. Or at least we were nothing more than best friends until about two months ago when he told me his feelings for me had changed and asked me to be his girlfriend. To say I was surprised when he told me how he felt would be an understatement. He dated a lot—a lot, a lot—and I was not his type. All his previous girlfriends were cheerleaders and sorority girls.

And all those women made sense since he's the quarterback for the University of Minnesota, where we go to school. He's so good that he's already been scouted to go pro. While I'm getting my degree in marine biology with plans to attend veterinary school when I'm finished. I've been his nerdy counterpart throughout our lives, and he's loved me anyway.

A sob I can't control climbs up the back of my throat, and I cry, not because I just lost my boyfriend, but because I know I just lost my best friend. Nothing between us will ever be the same. I cry until I can't anymore, then lay there wide awake, trying to figure out what I'm going to do. When the sun comes up, I pick up my cell phone, ignoring all the messages on the screen from Kirk, and make a phone call.

Chapter 1

Reese

With the balcony doors open, I look out at the ocean and breathe in the sea breeze. Three months ago, I would never have imagined that this would be the view I'd be waking up to every day. Then everything happened with Kirk and Melissa, and I knew staying in Minnesota wasn't an option. If I'm honest, I knew that long before all the drama.

Since our parents started dating, Melissa and I have had issues, but I always chalked it up to all the differences in our personalities. I'm more of a bookworm, and she's more Barbie. I like to stay home. She likes to spend her days shopping and her nights partying. None of that would have mattered if my mom hadn't had us move in with Richard and Melissa after Richard proposed. Or it wouldn't have mattered if I weren't stuck living in Melissa's dad's house while going to college, her in her second year, and me in my fourth and on the verge of graduating.

The morning I caught Melissa and Kirk together, I called my aunt Ileana—my dad's sister—who lives in Florida, and asked if I could stay with her while I figured things out. Thankfully, she agreed immediately. After I talked to her, I called my mom to let her know I would be moving. To say she was upset would be an understatement, especially when I refused to give her a reason why.

I just couldn't bring myself to tell her that Kirk and Melissa were sleeping together behind my back, not when she's loved Kirk for as long as I have.

I also didn't want to potentially cause any problems between her and Richard by telling her what his daughter did. Not that it was all

Melissa's fault. I mean, Kirk could have—and *should have*—said no. If he had wanted to be with Melissa, he could have been honest with me.

It would have been weird, but his betrayal wouldn't have blindsided me.

After talking to my aunt and Mom, I spoke to the college counselor to see what I needed to do to transfer schools. He basically told me that even though he understood my desire to move, something I made clear was a dire situation, it wasn't smart. I only had two months before I graduated, and I might not be able to do that if I decided to transfer.

After that conversation, I knew that even if it sucked, I needed to stay put. Which sucked more since I had already told my mom I was moving, and my aunt and I had made plans for me to get down to her.

The good thing was that one of my friends had a room available in the small condo her parents had bought for her and offered it to me.

After sorting out a place to stay, I called my aunt back, told her my new plan, and lived with Hellen for two months as I finished school, ignored Kirk, avoided—or mostly avoided—my mom, and totally avoided her fiancé and his daughter. Then, as soon as I got my walking papers, I got in my car and drove to Florida. I didn't even take the time to walk across the stage before I left.

So, I've been here for a month, have sent off my application to get into the marine veterinary program at the University of Miami, and will hopefully find out soon if I'll be attending school in the fall. In the meantime, I'm working at the aquarium, which I love.

Even though my heart still hurts because I lost my best friend, and I hate the new rift between my mom and me because I can't tell her the truth about what happened—and she feels like I abandoned her for no reason—I get to wake up to the gorgeous view out the balcony doors in my bedroom every day and work with all the sea life I've been fascinated with since I was little. I also get the joy of being around my aunt, who didn't have kids of her own but loves me like I'm hers. She has since I was little, and she gave me even more love when my dad—her twin brother—passed away when I was only two.

With that thought, I toss back the blanket covering me and walk to the bathroom. My aunt's condo in Miami is stunning and seriously spacious. It has three bedrooms, three and a half baths, an office, kitchen, dining room, and two huge balconies—one off the kitchen and living room, and the other off two of the three bedrooms.

down to the pool. Surprising me, he waits until I'm done, and then the two of us walk side by side to the door that leads into the building. When we get to the elevator, I press the button for my floor, and he presses his, which I notice is for one of the penthouses at the top. When the doors close, the smell of his cologne or whatever soap he uses fills the small, enclosed space. It's difficult not to feel awkward being alone with him, especially when he only has on a pair of shorts that hang low on his hips.

When I finally reach my floor, I mentally sigh in relief and hurry to get off the elevator like it's on fire.

"Reese," he calls, and I spin around to find him leaning slightly out of the elevator with a look on his face that says he's trying not to laugh at something. "Since I don't have your phone number, I'll meet you in the lobby downstairs in an hour."

"Oh, yeah, okay. Sounds good." I hear him chuckle as he disappears back into the elevator. Ignoring the nervous butterflies flying around in my stomach, I rush down the hall to my aunt's apartment and use the key card to let myself inside.

My aunt did very well for herself, just like my dad had before he passed away in a car accident. When she was eighteen, my aunt left Sacramento, where she and my dad had grown up with my grandparents and moved to Los Angeles with aspirations of becoming a movie star. She never made it to the big screen, but for twenty-six years, she was on one of those daytime TV shows with all the drama and love triangles. And she had a leading role until the show was canceled when she was in her forties. Now, she does some modeling here and there, which isn't a surprise since she's gorgeous.

After brushing my teeth, I leave my bedroom and go to the kitchen, the smell of strong coffee permeating the air. Going right to the pot, I pour myself a cup, dump in some sugar and cream, then grab a bowl for cereal.

"Good morning, my beautiful girl," Aunt Ileana greets. Her Spanish accent isn't very thick but it is still noticeable as she drifts into the kitchen, the brightly colored dress she's wearing floating around her frame. Like always, she looks like she's ready to step onto the set to perform a scene. Her dark hair is perfectly curled, and her makeup is done to perfection.

"Morning, *tu tiá*." I smile as she stops to kiss me on the cheek, probably leaving her red lipstick behind. "Are you excited for your trip?" I ask, dumping cereal into my bowl as she walks over to pour herself a cup of coffee.

"I'm packed." Her smile is sad. "Are you sure you can't come with us? It's not too late."

"I need to work," I remind her—and myself, because tagging along with her to Paris, Rome, and London while she works and travels for two months would be magical. And I know from traveling with her in the past that I would have zero regrets.

"Next time," she says.

"Yes, hopefully," I agree. "Plus, someone needs to be here to keep Mickey company." I glance over at her fat white cat as he saunters into the kitchen, taking in the black at his ears and on the top of his head.

"He would be okay with James and Tony downstairs." She smiles at him when he falls to his bottom next to his empty wet-food dish, likely having eaten earlier this morning. "So,"—her eyes meet mine—"what are you going to do while I'm gone?"

"Work."

She scrunches her nose. "You need to live a little, Reese. Work is good, but you're young. You need to enjoy yourself and your life. Maybe hang by the pool or go to the beach. You could even find a handsome man to spend some time with." Her eyes wander over my face. "You're so beautiful, so young. You shouldn't let that go to waste."

"Maybe." I lie because the only thing I plan on doing in the weeks she'll be gone is catching up on all the books I've missed out on while studying for finals, and vegging out in front of the TV when I'm not working.

"At least agree to go to the pool. Get some sun and fresh air."

"I can do that," I give in, taking my bowl and coffee to the counter and pulling out a stool. "What time is Marco getting here?" Marco is Ileana's boyfriend, or her partner as she refers to him. They've been together for fifteen years, have never lived together, and she says they never will. She was married in her early twenties, and her husband was a jerk. Not only was he controlling, but he was also abusive, and none of that abuse started until after they were married and living together. By that time, their lives were so tangled it was difficult for her to just walk away. Years after she finally divorced him, she met Marco, and before things ever got serious, she let him know that she never wanted to get married or live with a man again. And since they're still together fifteen years later and one of the happiest couples I have ever seen, I have to assume their arrangement works for them.

"He should be here any minute now," she says, right as I hear the front door open. I lean back in my chair to watch Marco walk in wearing a dress shirt and slacks with a single piece of luggage I know, at least from the print covering it, is very expensive. While he sets it next to the door, I take him in. He's pretty. Not handsome or beautiful, but *pretty* with his pitch-black hair, darker complexion from his Dominican heritage, bright sea-green eyes, thick lashes, strong jaw, and perfect facial hair. Literally *perfect*. Like he takes time to style it.

"Good morning, princess," he greets me with a smile as he walks toward the kitchen.

"Morning." I grin and tip my head to the side to accept the cheek kiss I know is coming.

"Morning, *mi amor*." Aunt Ileana smiles when he comes out of his bend and walks toward her. Then, with the two of them looking like a clip from a movie, he wraps his arm around her waist, bends her over it, and kisses her. Smiling to myself, I shove a spoonful of cereal into my mouth.

"Are you packed?" he asks her, taking the cup from her hand to take a sip of her coffee.

"Yes, my bags are in my room."

"How many?" he asks with a grin.

She rolls her eyes. "Only three."

"Only three." His smile widens. "I'm going to need to rent a plane just for your luggage."

"We're away for almost two months."

"Yes, and in that time, you'll shop every day, and I'll have to buy you two more pieces of luggage for all your new stuff."

"Are you complaining?" She rests her hand on her hip.

"Never." He kisses her cheek and then looks at me. "What are your plans while we are gone?"

"Work," I repeat, sticking to my earlier statement and then glancing at my aunt when she makes a noise. I roll my eyes. "And the pool." Marco grins, probably knowing my aunt already talked to me. I look between the two of them. "Are you sure you don't want me to drive you to the airport?"

"The driver is already downstairs waiting," Marco tells me, stepping away from my aunt after handing back her mug. "I should go grab your things."

She watches him leave and then looks at me as she walks to the sink to rinse her cup. "Remember, Rosie will be here Tuesdays and Fridays to clean and pick up any groceries you need."

"I remember." I don't even bother telling her I can clean up and shop for myself while she is out of town. I offered to do those things when I moved in, and she explained that with the work she does for my aunt and a few other families in the building, Rosie takes care of her daughter, who needs extra care, and depends on every penny she makes.

"Ready, my love?" Marco calls from the door, and I slide off my stool to stand and give my aunt a hug.

"I love you." She wraps her arms around me. "Make sure you don't spend all your time inside."

"I won't."

She leans back to look me in the eye. "If you hear that you got accepted into the program, I expect a call."

"You'll be the first," I assure her, giving her one last hug before walking with her to the door to say goodbye to Marco. Once they're gone and the door is closed behind them, I walk back to the kitchen to clean up. When I'm done, I carry my coffee out to the balcony and take a seat on one of the loungers. I look down at the ocean and the people beginning to gather on the beach. Even from up here, I can hear the buzz of happiness in the air. When did I last have fun or step outside my comfort zone? *Never* would probably be the truthful answer. I let out a sigh. Maybe my aunt was right. Maybe I do need to live a little.

Chapter 2

Brodie

Lounging at the pool's edge with my shades on and earbuds in, I listen to my agent drone on about some projects I have coming up with a few brands. Years ago, I would have been thrilled by the idea of representing some sports drink or clothing brand. Now, I despise every second of the extra shit I need to do to stay relevant. *Relevant* is a term Doug uses, not me. I'd say my ability to score while on the ice keeps me pretty fucking relevant. He'd disagree. And does so regularly.

"So, I'll meet you in New York in two weeks for the shoot. If you need, I can find you a date for the fundraiser."

"I don't need you to do that," I grumble. He sighs, probably because he knows I'll show up solo. I have zero desire to date right now. I'm not even interested in having a woman on my arm for a night.

"Brodie." He exhales an annoyed breath.

"Doug." I smile.

"Fine. If you need me, you have my cell."

"Yeah, talk with you later." I end the call and then glance to my left when I see movement out of the corner of my eye.

With my sunglasses on, I watch the cute little brunette I clocked when I came out to hang by the pool get up from her lounger next to mine. I didn't notice her because she's the most stunning woman out here—not that she's not beautiful. She is. I noticed her because she was reading a book with a strange-looking fish on the cover, unlike the twelve I'd seen with flowers and a few with couples or single men. I also noticed her because she's the only woman under the age of forty not wearing a bikini. After placing her book on her chair, she adjusts her swimsuit, which looks like something Pamela Anderson wore during the height of *Baywatch*. Biting her bottom lip, she looks around and then peers at her stuff. I can almost hear her silently debating with herself, wondering if she should leave her things. This pool and the connected bar are private to the building, but that doesn't mean everyone here lives here full time. People rent out their homes or have family who use the facilities. She likely knows that.

"I'll watch them." Startled, her sunglass-covered gaze flies to mine. "If you want to go to the bar or restroom, I'm here and will watch your stuff while you're gone."

"Are you sure?"

"Yeah, I got you."

"Thanks. I'll be right back." She starts to walk off but stops and spins back to face me, jerking her thumb over her shoulder. "Do you want a water or something?"

"I'm good." I smile, caught off guard by the offer.

With a nod, she walks toward the bar at the edge of the pool. I watch her noticing a group of guys who have been drinking since I arrived an hour ago—and probably long before that—take notice of her. Three in the group start egging one of them on while pointing in her direction. I can't hear what they're saying, but they're obviously trying to get their friend to go over and talk to her. Not that it looks like he needs the encouragement.

With a cocky smirk, he gets out of the pool with his friends, laughing and acting like a bunch of drunk idiots, then starts his approach after a douchey grin over his shoulder to the guys.

My gaze goes to where she is now standing at the bar. The moment he's close to her, he reaches for her, placing his hand on her lower back. Jumping in surprise, she looks up at him and then takes a step away, dislodging his touch. When he says something, she shakes her head with a polite smile. He must say something else because she shakes her head again. With a frown, he glances toward his friends, shouting from the pool, then grins and closes the space between them once more. She takes a step back when he reaches out to touch her arm.

Annoyed because it's obvious she doesn't want his attention, and he's not backing down, I set aside my cell and get up. The closer I get, the clearer I hear him trying to coerce her into letting him buy her a drink. With her sunglasses now on the top of her head, I can see that she is starting to panic because he's not giving up.

I walk up to her and get in her space, shoving my sunglasses up, too. "Hey, baby." I look down at her, wrapping my arm around her waist and ignoring the shock etched into her pretty features. Jesus, she's cute. And without her sunglasses, I can see that her eyes are an unusual brown with gold near the center. "Did you already order your drink?"

"Umm," she whispers, looking adorably confused.

I can't help but grin. "I changed my mind about the water."

"Hey, man."

My smile slides away as I turn my head, leveling my gaze on the guy behind me. He visibly swallows. "Can I help you?"

"I..." He blinks, and then his brows come together like he's trying to figure something out.

If he wasn't wasted, he might say he recognizes me. But in the state he's in, and with the stench of alcohol coming off him, I doubt he'd recognize his own mother if she was standing right in front of him.

I don't pull my gaze off his as I order. "Get our drinks, babe, so we can get back to our chairs."

She steps away from me, sliding out of my hold, and I listen to her order two bottles of water.

The guy glances back at his friends, who are now watching the two of us. Then his eyes meet mine. "Do I know you?"

"I doubt it."

He shakes his head like the action will clear some of the fog. "You look familiar."

"Yeah, I get that a lot." I turn my back on him and get in her space again. Once she has the two bottles of water, I walk her back around the pool to our loungers, hovering my hand over her lower back but not touching her.

"You okay?" I ask softly when we reach our chairs. She lets out a long breath.

"Yeah." She glances at the guys in the pool, their friend back with them now. All of them are watching us. "Thanks for saving me," she whispers.

"Anytime." I put my sunglasses back on and sit, watching her pick her bag off the ground and start putting her book inside. "Don't let them make you leave," I tell her quietly, and she glances over at me. "If you wanna go, that's fine. But don't leave because of them." Biting her full bottom lip, she nods once and places her bag on the pool deck, taking a seat with her book on her thighs. "What are you reading?"

"*World Beneath*," she answers without looking at me and opens to the page her bookmark is holding.

"What's it about?"

"Marine biology," she answers again without looking up.

"That's an interesting choice of reading material." Honestly, with the title, I thought it might be some fantasy or sci-fi book.

She turns my way. "I'm hoping to get into the marine veterinary program here."

"Really?"

Really."

"That's cool as fuck," I mutter, and she flashes a small smile. "Do you live here?"

She nods. "I just moved to Miami."

"Me, too. Where did you move from?"

"Minnesota."

"Seriously?"

"Did you move from there, too?"

"No, Tennessee," I say. She laughs, and the sound makes me smile. "I said 'seriously' because it's rare that I meet someone from Minnesota."

"I guess." She leans back in her seat, raises her knees, and presses her feet into her chair. "So, why did you move to Florida?"

"Work," I say simply and leave it at that. I don't think she recognizes me. Then again, she could be one of those women who thinks pretending they don't know who you are will score them points. It doesn't. In the long run, it's just annoying.

"Cool," she mutters, turning her attention to the book on her lap. I frown at her easy dismissal.

Chapter 3

Reese

I knew moving from Minnesota to Florida would be an adjustment, but I assumed the weather would be the biggest thing I'd have to get used to. I was wrong. It's the people, or more accurately, the number of drunk jerks who come to party for the weekends and believe every woman on the beach, by the pool, or just out and about is seeking their attention. We're not. Or, at least, I'm not. The guy from earlier wasn't the first to hit on me without me giving them the slightest inkling that I was interested. The first time I came to the pool, I wore a bikini and stupidly thought that was the reason for the unwanted attention. After today, I realize it's just because I'm female.

I look at the guy lying next to me out of the corner of my eye and feel the heat rise to my cheeks when my eyes connect with his muscular, tan torso. When he first came out of the building, I noticed him the same way all the other women did. It was difficult not to. He's gorgeous with his dark hair, chiseled jaw, broad shoulders, and lean, muscular frame. For a moment, I thought I recognized him, but it was only because he looked like he would play the leading hero in some action movie or be on a billboard in Times Square. I never would have expected him to come rescue me from the guy at the bar like some kind of white knight. But if he hadn't come over to save me, there is a chance I would have let that guy in the pool buy me a drink just so he'd back off. Because me telling him, "no thank you," the three times he asked hadn't worked.

Turning my attention back to my book and finding the words on the page not penetrating, I decide to just close it. Placing it on top of my bag, I sit up and adjust my chair so I can lay it flat and then lie down on my stomach. I wish I could say my aunt was wrong and that getting some sun on my days off doesn't make me feel good, but it does. There is something about the warmth on my skin that I've come to appreciate.

"Have you been to the aquarium here?" Opening one eye, I look at the guy next to me and find his chin dipped, and his aviators on me.

I'd thought his one-word answer for why he's living in Miami was his cue that our conversation was over.

"I work there."

"You work at the aquarium?"

"I do. I work with the sea lions and dolphins. Have you been?"

"Not since I was a kid."

"You need to go back. I'm sure a lot has changed in the last thirty years."

"Thirty?" He grins.

"It's just a guess." I can't help my smile.

"So, you think I look old."

"Mature." I lift my feet behind me. "I think you look mature."

"I'm only thirty-two."

"Oh, so you *are* old." I grin as he laughs.

"How old are you?"

"I turned twenty-five a few weeks ago."

"You're a baby."

"Compared to you, yeah."

"She's got jokes," he mutters with a smile that makes my stomach feel weird. "So, you're twenty-four and starting the marine veterinary program here. That's a pretty big deal."

"Hoping to start. I haven't been accepted yet," I remind him.

"What is your grade-point average?"

"Four."

"Jesus, you're smart. With that average, you'll get in."

"I hope so," I mumble, ignoring the warmth in my cheeks.

"What is your plan if you don't get in?" he asks.

I freeze, every muscle locking up. I haven't thought about that once. I should have. I should have applied to other schools and thought about what I'd do if I don't get accepted. "I don't know," I whisper.

"Hey," he calls, and my gaze goes to him. "You'll get in."

"I should have applied to other schools."

"Why didn't you?"

"Because this is the best program, and I..." I shake my head. "I don't know what I was thinking." I sit up. "Maybe it's not too late to apply to a few other places." I dig through my bag for my phone so I can check and see when the cutoff date is for some of the other schools. When I finally find my cell in one of the side pockets, the screen lights up with a few notifications. Some for my email, one for my single social media account, and another a text from Kirk.

Kirk: *Reese I'm heading to New York in two weeks to move into my new place then training camp in July. Please message me back when you have time.*

I don't respond. I never do. But that doesn't mean the part of me that has been his best friend since we were kids isn't proud of him. Before I left Minnesota in April, it was all over campus that he got drafted by a team in New York. And from his message, it's obvious he's getting ready to move and start training for the NFL. Part of me wants so badly to hear his voice and share in his excitement, but there's still too much anger wrapped around what happened between us for me to take that step.

After I delete his message, I go to my email and scroll through the list. Not surprisingly, they're all spam. I delete them and am about to exit and open the browser, but I freeze when an email from Miami pops up.

"No way, they just emailed me," I whisper to myself, feeling the guy on the lounger next to mine move. His shadow falls over me.

"Who? The college?"

I lift my head, and our sunglass-covered eyes lock. "Yes."

"Open it."

My stomach churns. "I can't."

"Do you want me to do it?"

With a nod, I hand the guy—who is basically a stranger—my phone and watch him shove his aviators up into his thick, dark hair.

As he stares at whatever is written, my heart pounds. Then, his blue eyes meet mine.

"Well?"

Ducking his head, he starts to read.

"Dear Reese Shepard. Congratulations and welcome…"

"Oh, my God." I cover my mouth with my hand and shoot up off the lounger. "I'm in?"

"You're in." He grins at me, and I have the oddest urge to hug him.

"Oh, my God," I say again, falling to my bottom and taking my phone when he holds it out to me. "I can't believe it." I read the email that talks about how I was selected and saying I will receive my official decision in the mail, along with the information I need to finish enrollment.

"How are you going to celebrate?"

I look at him once more. "I don't know. Maybe I'll order pizza and watch a movie."

"Alone?"

"My aunt is... My aunt is working today, and my mom doesn't live here." No way am I telling a stranger that I'm basically living alone.

"Then I'm taking you out."

"What?" I laugh.

"I'm not going to let you celebrate your accomplishment alone." He stands. "It's four. How long will it take you to get ready to go out to dinner?"

"Um." I glance around, wondering if I'm being punked. "I don't know."

"Is an hour good for someplace casual with good food?"

"Are you being serious?"

"Yes." He smiles, and I shake my head.

"I don't even know your name."

"Brodie." I don't think I've ever met a Brodie before, but the name suits him.

Biting my lip, I debate taking him up on his offer. Normally, I would say no, but I just shared a huge moment with him and can actually hear a little voice in the back of my head telling me I should go. And honestly, I can't think of a reason not to. It's dinner out. He didn't ask me to go back to his place for a drink. Maybe, like me, he doesn't know anyone here and is looking for people to connect with.

"Okay."

"Okay?" He raises a brow.

"Yes, dinner sounds good."

"All right." I watch him begin to gather his towel and phone from the table on the opposite side of his lounger while I pack my things into my bag and shrug on the simple cotton dress I wore over my swimsuit

Chapter 4

Brodie

Standing in the lobby of the building, I watch the elevator for Reese while ignoring the group of women gathered on one of the couches near the entrance. All five are dressed similarly in barely-there dresses and short shorts, whispering among each other while doing a horrible job of not making it obvious they're talking about me.

It's weird to think that I used to feed off that kind of thing—feed off women throwing themselves at me and the constant attention. Then, I lost the only woman besides my mom that I'd ever loved because I craved the ego boost the other women gave me. I didn't take my ex seriously when she told me that the flirting bothered her, even if it was innocent. I thought she was being dramatic. Looking back, I realize I expected her to put up with it because of who I am. It was stupid. *I* was stupid and immature.

"Hey." I turn my head and look down at the blonde who broke away from her friends to approach me. "Are you Brodie Larsen?"

"No, sorry," I deny, and she frowns, glancing back at her friends before looking at me once more.

"Are you sure?"

"Yeah, sorry." I give her a smile so I don't come off like a dick, then turn to the elevator when I hear the ding of the doors opening. With my hands tucked into the pockets of my shorts, I watch a group of people step off and then see Reese following behind them. I don't know why I thought she would look completely different. Maybe because I'm used to women going all out with hair and makeup. But she's as cute as she was by the pool, maybe even cuter with her glasses and her hair down, dressed casually in a pair of jean shorts with a tank top and sandals. Looking around, she fidgets awkwardly, and I can't help but smile.

"Reese," I call, and she turns my way. Her shoulders seem to sag in relief as soon as our gazes lock. Yeah, she's cute.

"Hey." She walks toward me with a small smile. "Sorry I'm late; the elevator took forever."

"It's all good." I motion with my chin toward the door. "Are you ready to go eat?"

"Yes, I'm starving. Do you know where you want to go?"

"I figured we'd walk down the street and stop wherever sounds good if that works."

"Totally." I shorten my stride, and she falls into step beside me.

"Did you share the news of your acceptance with anyone?"

"I called my aunt." She tips her head back to look up at me. "She's happy for me, and I left a message for my mom. I haven't heard back from her yet."

"I'm sure she will be proud."

"Probably." She shrugs as I wrap my hand around her elbow to maneuver her around a crowd of people gathered in the middle of the sidewalk. When we reach one of the first restaurants, I stop at the menu posted outside.

"Do you like Italian?" I look down at her.

"I do," she says, but her attention goes a bit farther down the street. "But there's a Greek place down a little ways that is supposed to be really good." Her gaze meets mine once more. "Do you like Greek food?"

"I love all food."

"Do you mind if we check out the menu there?"

"Not at all." We fall into step once more. When we get to the restaurant, she takes her time looking at the menu. "What do you think?"

"I don't know." She looks up and down the street. "I'm so hungry everything sounds good, and now I can't decide if I want a gyro, pasta primavera, or a burger from the spot down the street I order from sometimes."

"Pick a number between one and three."

Her pretty brown eyes meet mine. "Two."

"Greek, it is." Her nose scrunches, making me laugh. "You don't want a gyro?"

She looks at the menu we're still in front of, then at me. "Maybe you should just pick; otherwise, we might never eat."

"All right." I take her elbow and walk with her past two more restaurants to a diner I know offers almost every kind of food item you could ask for. My teammates and I went there one night after hanging out and drinking. "Have you been here?" I ask when we stop at the podium at the front.

"No, never. Is the food good?"

"Yeah, and they have a huge menu, so you should be able to find something." I hover my hand over her lower back when the girl at the front takes us to one of the booths and then wait for her to sit before sliding into my seat.

After we order drinks—her a Coke and me just water—I watch her look over the menu, already knowing what I'll get.

"Do you want to share an appetizer?"

"Sure," I agree, and she sets her menu aside. "What did you decide on?"

"The French dip." She smiles when I laugh.

"Is your mom back in Minnesota?" I ask after the waitress comes over with our drinks and takes our orders.

"Yeah, she lives there with her fiancé and his daughter."

"Where is your dad?"

Her expression falls slightly. "He passed away when I was young."

"I'm sorry."

"It was a long time ago."

"Time doesn't always make it easier."

"You're right about that." Her smile is sad.

"So, if your mom is back in Minnesota, who do you know here?" I ask to change the subject and to get that sad look out of her eyes.

"My aunt Ileana," she says as the waitress comes over to drop off the mozzarella sticks Reese ordered for an appetizer.

"Are you two close?"

"Yeah. She and my dad were twins, and with my dad gone, we only got closer over the years." Her smile is fond. "She's kind of always been like a second mom to me. I obviously lived with my real mom, but when

I was growing up, I would fly to California, where my aunt was living at the time, and spend my summers with her. Or if I had a long break from school, she would come to Minnesota to visit, or we would travel."

"That's cool."

"She's the best." She picks up a cheese stick, tears it in half, and then blows on it as she looks at me. "What about your family?"

"My parents live in Kentucky. I have a brother who lives in Chicago with his wife and my niece, who just turned two. And a sister who just moved to Nashville to live with her boyfriend."

"Why did you say *boyfriend* like that?" she asks, covering her mouth with her hand as she chews.

"I don't like him. He's self-centered and thinks he's God's gift. My sister could do better, but she likes the lifestyle he offers, so she's put up with a bunch of shit she shouldn't have had to."

I watch her nose scrunch. "Does she love him?"

"She says she does."

"Then you'll never change her mind about him, and if you try, it will just create a rift between the two of you."

"You say that like you know from experience."

"My mom's fiancé isn't her first boyfriend since my dad died." She shrugs. "Mom likes living a life of leisure and travel, and over the years, she's found man after man to give that to her. Not to say she didn't care about them, but until Richard, I don't think she was ever in love. She just appreciated the fact that those men could take care of her. And for her, that's what's most important." She picks up another mozzarella stick.

"When I was a teenager, I would get so mad at her, and we would fight all the time about it. I knew the men she was with before Richard weren't treating her right, and I couldn't understand why she kept seeking out the same kind of men over and over again." Her eyes lock on mine. "Nothing changed except our relationship. She always felt like I was judging her when I wasn't. I just wanted better for her, even if it was a better kind of man."

"But you like her fiancé now?"

"He treats her like a princess and worships the ground she walks on. That's really all that matters to me."

"Do you and he get along?"

"Yeah." She shrugs. "But I honestly can't say I know him well, which is weird since I lived in his house for almost six months after he proposed to my mom."

"How is that possible?"

"He travels all the time for work and was gone more than he was around."

"That has to be difficult on your mom."

"She goes with him." She takes another mozzarella stick, and I watch her eat it, thinking even the way she eats is cute. "So, what about your parents?"

"My mom works for the FBI," I say.

"Wait, what?" She laughs. "Are you serious?"

"Yeah, but she's not an agent. She works in the office, which isn't as exciting."

"Maybe, but you still get to say your mom works for the FBI." She laughs again.

"True." I grin and then lean back when the waitress brings over our food.

"What about your dad?" She grabs the ketchup.

"He was a car salesman but retired a few years ago. Now, he spends his days fishing."

"I love fishing," she says softly, the look in her eyes matching the tone of her voice.

"Really?" I raise a brow.

"Three of my favorite things are fishing, scary movies, and baking cookies."

Chapter 5

Reese

Taking my eyes off the sandwich I just picked up, I look across the table at Brodie, who's suddenly gone quiet, and try to figure out why he seems... Annoyed?

"What?"

"Are you being serious right now?"

"That I like fishing?" I dunk my sandwich into the bowl of au jus. "Yeah, why? Do you think that's weird?"

"And the other things?"

"Scary movies and baking?" I frown at him. Why does he keep looking at me like that?

"Do you know who I am?"

"Should I?" I let my eyes wander over his face. Did I actually recognize him this afternoon like I thought I had? Is he some famous actor or something? "Are you famous?"

"I play pro hockey."

"You play hockey? For like a job?"

He jerks up his chin.

"I don't watch hockey," I say.

"So, you never read the article about me that came out two months ago in *LifeNStylez*, where I said that my three favorite things are fishing, scary movies, and baking?"

"I've never even heard of that magazine." I shake my head, trying to wrap my mind around the last thing he said. "You like baking?"

"I'm being serious right now, Reese. I'm trying to figure out if this is all just some strange coincidence or if…"

It clicks. Right then, in that moment, it clicks. The weird look on his face, the way he seems freaked, maybe even a little mad.

"Oh, my God. You think I'm some weird stalker fan," I breathe in disbelief.

"I didn'—"

"How would I even go about that?" I ask with zero humor, placing my sandwich on the plate and dusting off my hands.

"I don't know." He scrubs his fingers through his hair.

"Right." I pick up my bag from beside me, ready to bolt. "Before I leave, I would just like to point out that I didn't sit by you at the pool. You sat by me. I didn't try to talk to you; you talked to me. And I didn't ask you to dinner; you asked me. So, unless I enthralled you with my beauty and wit and have some kind of magical power that manipulated you into doing all those things, I don't see how you'd think that I set this whole situation up." I start to stand but stop when he gets there before me and blocks my path.

"You're right," he says quietly, looking down at me. "I'm sorry, it's just…"

"Let me guess, women are constantly throwing themselves in your path or trying to find ways to get your attention."

"Something like that," he mutters, looking uncomfortable. I have to admit, I feel a little bad for him if his first assumption about having a few things in common with someone is that they dug up that information from somewhere and are trying to play him.

"Don't go, okay? I shouldn't have assumed you'd do something like that," he pleads. "It was wrong of me to think that."

"Very wrong."

"Very wrong," he agrees. Then asks quietly, "Are you staying?"

I nod and then wait for him to retake his seat across from me.

"Do you really like baking, or is that something you made up so women would find you endearing?"

"No, I enjoy it. It's relaxing." He picks up his burger and meets my gaze. "You really like fishing?"

"I love it, or rather, I love ice fishing. My—" I cut myself off.

"Your?"

"When I was growing up, I would go with my best friend's dad and him almost every weekend in the winter. There is something magical about being in that little hut, waiting for a fish we would cook right there after pulling it out of the water." I shrug. "I haven't gone in a long time, but that is one of my favorite memories from when I was a kid."

"Have you ever gone deep-sea fishing?"

"No, have you?"

"I go whenever I get the chance." His gaze wanders over my face. "What are you doing tomorrow?"

"Nothing. I have the day off."

"Do you want to go out fishing with me?"

"Are you serious?"

"I never joke about fishing."

"Then, yeah. That sounds like fun."

"All right." He sets his burger down and takes his cell phone out of his pocket. I watch him type something, and then he sets it aside and resumes eating until it dings a moment later. After he picks it up and checks the screen, his eyes meet mine. "Does eight work for you?"

"Sure." I dunk one of my fries into some ketchup.

Dropping his gaze, he quickly texts something back before lifting his burger once more. "We'll meet the charter company I use in the morning, and they'll take us out."

"It must be nice to be rich and famous," I joke, then cringe because it's obvious that who he is is a sensitive topic for him. "Sorry, I shouldn't have said that."

"Don't be." He shrugs. "I deal with that kind of shit from my family all the time."

"They give you a hard time about it?"

"Constantly." He smiles. "My brother is the worst."

"So, when you say you play pro hockey, I'm guessing that means you're pretty good."

"I don't suck." His smile is tinged with a bit of cockiness.

"I don't know much about hockey. How long have you been playing?"

"Since I was a kid. My dad bought me my first pair of skates when I was four. I joined my first team when I was seven and have been playing ever since. You'll have to come to a game when the season starts up."

"I'm not really a fan of sporting events." I hated watching Kirk play football, so I avoided his games like the plague, which probably made me a pretty crappy girlfriend. I just didn't enjoy the violent aspects of the sport and would sit there the whole time with a pit in my stomach, knowing that one wrong hit could cause irrevocable damage. And knowing what little I do about hockey, I imagine it would be the same thing.

"What sports do you like?"

"None." I tip my head to the side. "That's a lie. That sport they play in the Olympics, where they sweep that black ball thing with brooms down the ice, is pretty cool."

"Curling is not a sport."

"It's in the Olympics, so I'd guess they'd disagree with you on that topic."

I listen to him laugh, the deep sound just as attractive as he is, especially when his eyes crinkle at the corners. The dimple in his left cheek, which I didn't notice before, shows ever so slightly. Ignoring the flutter in my lower belly, I focus on eating and just enjoying his company.

Being friends is safe, but there is no way I'll entertain more than that with an apparently famous hockey player who has women throwing themselves at him.

Chapter 6

Brodie

Walking out of the cabin where the captain is, I take the stairs down to the lower deck and stop at the bottom, finding Reese where I left her, lying on one of the cushioned benches that encircle the front half of the boat. She's beautiful, with the sun shining down on her, making her brown hair appear more red. She also looks miserable and almost green, which I thought was a myth when people talked about getting seasick. She'd been fine on the hour ride out to our fishing spot, but about ten minutes after the boat came to a stop and the captain dropped the anchor, the look she gave me let me know she was going to be sick. Two seconds later, she leaned over the side of the boat and lost her breakfast.

As I walk toward her, she opens her eyes. "I'm sorry. I suck," she whispers, looking up at me pitifully.

"Stop apologizing." I squat in front of her and smooth her hair out of her face. "Are you feeling any better after the pill?"

"I want to say yes, but no. I'm pretty sure I'll be sick again if I move from this position."

"You don't need to move." I stand and then sit next to her head on the bench.

"I guess I should have thought about how different ice fishing is from deep-sea fishing. You know, one being on frozen water and the other not."

"I should have asked if you'd ever been on a boat." I rest my hand on her forehead—cool to the touch despite the sun.

"Yeah, come to think of it, this is definitely all your fault." Laughing, I look down at her. I haven't laughed so much in a very long time. Her humor and honesty are both refreshing. *She's* refreshing. And

I'm still annoyed at myself about yesterday when I basically accused her of stalking me.

"I know better for next time. I'll make sure to give you something to take before we get on the boat."

"There isn't going to be a next time. This was a one-time thing. I will never go out on another boat again."

"We'll see," I mutter, watching her try to keep her eyes open, which is probably difficult with the pill she took. One of the side effects was making you tired. "Try to sleep. You'll be on solid ground soon."

With a nod, she pulls the towel I gave her up and over her shoulder, then curls into a ball, tucking her knees into her stomach. I try to resist touching her, but it's difficult not to. It's also impossible not to stare at her. She fascinates me. I don't think any woman has ever fascinated me before.

When the boat finally reaches the dock and the bridge is in place, I attempt to wake Reese. But she's so out of it she says something I can't understand, and her lashes barely flutter open. With no choice, I stand and lift her into my arms, carrying her off the boat, down the dock, and to my truck that we came in together this morning. It's a feat getting her inside, and I have to admit that when I try to wake her once more and she doesn't budge, I'm a little concerned. I debate taking her to the hospital but decide to call my sister-in-law Maci, who is a nurse, instead.

"Brodie?" Maci answers on the second ring. "Everything okay?"

"I just have a quick question about Dramamine."

"What about it?"

"If someone took it, is it normal for them not to wake up?"

"Define not waking up," she says, sounding concerned. "Are they breathing?"

"Yes, she's breathing, just completely passed out."

"Some people have a more extreme reaction to diphenhydramine. Do you know if she is on any type of allergy medication?"

"I have no idea."

"When did she take the Dramamine?"

"A little over an hour ago."

"Give her a couple more hours. I'm sure she's fine."

"All right. Thanks, Maci."

"Anytime." We hang up after saying goodbye.

I glance over at Reese and then put my truck in reverse, heading toward our building. When we arrive, she is still totally out, so I carry her inside and ignore the strange looks I get from everyone I pass. Not knowing where she lives since we met in the lobby this morning, I have no choice but to take her up to my apartment. As soon as I get us inside, my Great Dane Jeb is there to greet us. Always curious, he refuses to give me an inch of space as I take her to the couch and put a blanket over her.

"Come on, bud, you'll meet her when she wakes up." I order him to follow me to the kitchen and then give him one of his chew bones that will hopefully keep him distracted for a while. If it fails, I have no doubt he'll be on the couch with her, and she'll wake up with seventy pounds of slobbering dog on her chest. Once I have him settled, I turn on the TV and plant myself on the sectional across from Reese, waiting for her to wake up.

* * * *

"Hey," I hear through my subconscious. Blinking my eyes open, my gaze connects with Reese's. She's leaning over me and still looks sleepy but also alert, and the color is back in her cheeks.

"You're awake." I sit up.

"Yeah." She laughs, looking at Jeb next to her. "Your friend woke me."

"Shit, sorry about that."

"It's okay. Can I use your restroom?"

"Of course. It's right around the corner on the left." I jerk my chin in the direction of the hall.

"Thanks." She gives me a smile and then turns on her heels. When Jeb starts to follow, I call him back. He has no regard for personal space and will follow her in there if she lets him.

Getting up, I walk to the kitchen and glance at the clock on the microwave. It's a little after one. When I pass the window that looks out at the ocean, I can see that the beach below is filled with people.

I grab the jug of water from the fridge and two glasses from the cabinet. When Reese walks around the corner into the living room a few minutes later, Jeb trots her way with his tail wagging.

"Hey, new friend." She pets his head when he shoves it into her stomach.

"That's Jeb."

"Jeb." She grins, taking his face in her hands. "You sure are handsome."

He woofs like he knows what she's saying, and she giggles, looking up and meeting my gaze.

"How are you feeling?"

"Great." She laughs. "I'm guessing you couldn't wake me up."

"You were out of it. I thought about taking you to the hospital, but I called my sister-in-law instead. She said you'd be fine but asked if you were on any allergy medication."

"I am."

"Apparently, that can affect how the Dramamine works."

"Now I know."

"Now you know," I agree. "Do you want some water?"

"No. I'll just get something at home since I'm starving."

"I have food. Or we can order in."

She studies me for a moment like she's debating taking me up on my offer, then shakes her head. "That's okay." Her smile is small. "I'll get out of your hair." She picks up her bag from the coffee table where I put it. "Thanks for taking care of me and for today. The boat ride was fun..." She wiggles her head from side to side. "Until it wasn't."

"Yeah." I laugh, scrubbing my fingers through my hair, at a loss for how to get her to stay—or why I want her to so badly. Sure, I'm attracted to her, but she honestly seems totally disinterested in me, and it's fucking with my head and making me question if I really like her or if I just like her because she seems almost unattainable.

With her bag in hand, she starts to the door. Of course, Jeb begins to follow. I walk behind them to stop him from getting out and then pause when she turns to face me.

"*Scream* is playing on the beach tomorrow night. I was thinking about going when I get home from work." She rubs her full lips together. "Would you want to go with me?"

"Yeah."

"Cool." She smiles. "I'll text you and let you know when I get home."

"Sounds good." I step around her, grab Jeb's collar, and then open the door. "I'll see you tomorrow."

"See you tomorrow." Of course, she stops to give my fucking dog a rubdown and a hug while I stand there and watch, then her eyes meet mine, and my stomach muscles clench. "Later."

"Later, Ree." That gets me another smile, and then she's gone. I close the door behind her and look down at Jeb, who looks like he's pouting while gazing at the closed door. Then he meets my eye, and I swear he glares. "Hey, don't look at me like that. I tried to get her to stay; she didn't want to." Letting out a huff, he turns his back to me and walks to the living room, sprawling out on the floor. "Are you so mad that you don't want to go for a walk?" I grab his leash, and he's instantly back up and dancing around my feet.

"Thought so." I laugh.

Chapter 7

Reese

With my cell pressed between my ear and shoulder, I walk into my closet wrapped in a towel to look for something to wear while listening to my mom tell me about the venue she found for her wedding. I'm only half-paying attention. Not because I don't care, but because I'm running late. I'm supposed to meet Brodie downstairs in less than ten minutes so we can go have dinner, something that has become a nightly ritual for us since we watched *Scream* together on the beach a week ago. I'm still not quite sure how it happened, but somehow, we've ended up with dinner plans every day this week.

"You'll be able to make it for the wedding, right?" my mom asks as I slip a simple black cotton summer dress over my head.

I squeeze my eyes closed as I adjust the thin straps at my shoulders. "Um. I…"

"Reese, it's my wedding. You can't honestly tell me you might miss it."

Guilt eats at my insides. "Mom."

"I know what happened." She drops her voice. "Melissa told me you got upset that she and Kirk were spending time together." I almost laugh… Almost. "You can't be mad that they're friends, Reese."

So, they're still friends? I don't ask.

"I would never be mad that they're friends or that they were spending time together." *I was angry that they were sleeping together behind my back.* I don't tell her that. I can't. "School starts in August. I haven't gotten my schedule yet, so I'm not sure. Plus, I still have to work."

"You know you don't need to work, Reese. Your dad made sure of that. Stop acting like you don't have any money."

"I'll let you know as soon as possible if I can make it or not," I say, ignoring her comment. My dad did leave me a very sizable trust fund, but school is expensive, and I don't want to be one of those people who looks back and wonders what happened to the money they had. As for Mom's wedding, it isn't even in Minnesota. The venue she found is in Hawaii, and that's not just a quick weekend trip. It takes planning. The plane ride alone is seventeen hours with a layover, which means I would have to plan for at least a five-day trip. Not to mention, I'm not sure I'm mentally ready to be around Melissa—and possibly Kirk—yet.

"All right." She sighs, sounding disappointed. "I love you."

"I love you, too. I'll call you soon." I hang up after saying goodbye and then walk back into my bathroom. After hanging up my towel, I check my reflection, then shove my feet into my flip-flops and head for the door, grabbing my purse on the way out.

When the elevator doors open on the ground floor a few minutes later, I immediately spot Brodie and, right on cue, those pesky butterflies with no sense of self-preservation take flight.

Ignoring them has gotten more difficult the more time Brodie and I spend together, but I'm determined.

As I wait for a couple with three kids and a stroller to get off the elevator ahead of me, I take him in. Standing with his arms crossed and a disinterested look on his face, his body language screams: *Do not approach*. I get it, or I'm starting to understand that he doesn't love the attention he gets just for being who he is. More than once while we were out, random people came up to talk to him. And although he's always friendly with the men who approach to say hi, the women are a different story. Or at least they are when they come up to him, breathing his name like they just finished having sex and are ready for another round. He dismisses them without much care.

When I finally get off the elevator, I step around the couple now trying to detain one of their little boys, who obviously has no desire to be strapped into the stroller his parents are attempting to lock him in.

Jeb is the first to notice my arrival and stands with a happy woof, wagging his tail. "Hey." I smile at him and then look up at Brodie. A warm, familiar smile replaces the disinterested look he wore moments ago.

"Took you long enough." He leans down to kiss my cheek, and my insides twist in response.

"Sorry. I was on the phone with my mom," I tell him, rubbing Jeb's head.

"Everything okay?" he asks as we fall into step and walk out of the building. Even with the sun not directly overhead, it's still hot.

"She was telling me about the wedding venue she found in Hawaii."

"Is that where she's getting married?"

"She's thinking about it. But if she does, I don't know if I will be able to go." I glance up at him. "She wants to have the wedding in August, but that's around the time school starts."

"That sucks."

"Yeah," I lie. Because if she does have her wedding in Hawaii in August, and I have a legit reason not to go, it will make my life so much easier.

"So, what are you in the mood for tonight?"

"Whatever you want." I shrug. With Jeb along, there are fewer options since we have to find a restaurant with an outdoor dining area. I don't mind. I enjoy having him with us, especially after dinner when we normally take him down to the beach to run for a bit.

"All right." Brodie wraps his hand around mine but then lets go quickly. "Sorry, habit."

Habit? Like he's used to holding someone's hand so often that he reached out for mine without thinking. My insides twist, and not in a good way.

Sitting across from him sometime later under a dark blue awning outside an Italian restaurant, I study him as he looks over the menu in his hand while Jeb lies under the table at our feet. We've spent a lot of time together this last week. And we often text throughout the day, so we've talked a lot, and about many things. But I've never asked him about his love life, and he's never asked me about mine. Is that weird? Should I know if he has a girlfriend, even if we're only friends?

"Do you have a girlfriend?" Shit, I know how that probably sounded. He lifts his gaze to mine. "Not that I'm interested." I hold up a hand. "I'm not. I'm just curious because you said *habit* earlier, like you're used to holding someone's hand."

"Jesus. You're horrible for my fucking ego, Ree."

Darn. I really love it when he calls me Ree. No one has ever given me a nickname before, and it's cute when he says it.

"Sorry."

"I don't have a girlfriend." Relief I have no reason to feel sweeps over me. "But I had one back in Tennessee."

"Did you break up because you were moving to Florida?"

"No. She broke up with me long before that because I was an idiot."

"Oh."

"Do you have a boyfriend?" He places his menu on the table, giving me his undivided attention. I shake my head. "When was your last relationship?"

Damn, I should have thought about how my question might be turned around on me. "A few months before I moved here," I say, thankful that I don't need to say more because the waitress shows up to take our orders.

"Okay," he starts when she wanders off a minute later. All hope of getting out of this conversation crashes and burns when he asks, "What happened with your ex?"

"You go first."

He leans back in his chair, studying me with an odd look. "I let my ego take up space in our relationship." I frown at him, not sure what that means. "She told me she wasn't comfortable with the amount of female attention I get, and I ignored her."

"Did you cheat on her?" I can't help the anger that seeps into my tone. And if he says yes, I will get up and walk away from this table without letting him explain.

"Fuck no. I would never have hurt her like that." He scrubs his fingers through his hair. "I was just a shitty boyfriend. I see it now, but at the time, I thought she was just insecure. And she was, but not for the reason I assumed. I didn't give her the attention she needed to let her know she was a priority. I didn't make her feel safe. I didn't tell women no when they wanted a picture or avoid the flirting that sometimes goes along with that. I didn't think it was a big deal. I knew it wasn't going anywhere and thought it was innocent." He shakes his head. "Like I said, my ego took up a lot of room in our relationship."

I chew the inside of my cheek now, understanding why his whole demeanor changed when women approached him.

"Now, you tell me what happened with your ex."

"I found out that he was sleeping with my soon-to-be stepsister."

His eyes widen. "He what?"

"It's not a big deal."

"Yeah, Ree, it is a big fucking deal. What the fuck?"

"Okay, you're right, it is a big deal." I let out a breath. "He was my best friend, and I don't mean that in the way some people talk about their partners. I mean, we were best friends since we were little, and only got together a couple of months before he slept with her, and I moved. I…" I shake my head. "It's funny."

"What is?"

"I knew before we even got together that a relationship between us wouldn't work. I knew from watching him date that I was nothing like the other women he had been with. But he was so adamant that he wanted to be in a relationship with me that I got scared and gave in because I didn't want to lose him." I shake my head. "Then I lost him anyway."

"How were you different than the other women he dated?"

"They were all beautiful and peppy cheerleaders or sorority girls. That just isn't me."

"You're gorgeous, Ree." I give him a doubt-filled look, and not because I'm vying for a compliment. I don't think I'm ugly, but *gorgeous* is not a word anyone has ever used to describe me. I've been cute since I was little. "The first time I saw you, I thought you were beautiful. And in a world filled with sorority girls, you stand out because you're just you with your nerdy books and ability to be brutally honest and funny as fuck."

"Thank you." It seems like a stupid reply, but the words slip off the tip of my tongue while my heart flutters behind my rib cage.

Darn. When his gaze softens like it did just now, it's hard to remember why I shouldn't want more than just his friendship.

"I have a question."

"Okay." I pick up my water and take a sip.

"Do you work next weekend, or can you take off?"

"I don't work Saturday or Sunday. It's my one weekend off this month."

"Perfect. Do you want to go with me to New York?"

"New York?" My brows drag together.

"I have a fundraiser I need to attend Saturday night, and I need a date."

"And you want me to go with you? As your date?"

"There is no one else I'd want to go with. And if you don't go with me, I'm going alone."

"I…"

"I'll make sure you have your own room, and we can explore the city after my shoot on Saturday afternoon."

"Your shoot?"

"I have to do a photo shoot for this new sports drink that's about to hit the market."

"Is it any good?"

"I haven't tried it. They sent me a case, but it's still sitting next to the front door in my apartment."

"So, you're going to advertise something that might taste like dirty bath water?" The look he gives me makes me laugh. "You at least need to try it, Brodie."

"After we get done with dinner and take Jeb to the beach, we'll taste-test it."

"We can do that."

"So, will you go with me?"

I don't know if it's the hope-filled look in his eyes or my aunt's voice in the back of my head telling me I should live a little, but I say, "Yes." It comes out before my brain can really catch up. Darn, did I really just agree to go with him to New York? His smile says I did, and my heart flutters once again.

"I'll take care of everything. Just let me know your schedule for Friday, and I'll have my assistant book our flights so we can be together."

"It will probably be late by the time I get off work."

"That's okay. I'll wait for you."

I nod. "Do I need a fancy dress for this fundraiser?"

"Yes, it's black tie."

"Fun," I lie, and he laughs.

"Just let me know when you find your dress and I'll give you the money for it."

"We'll figure that out later," I mutter, knowing there is no way I'm letting him pay for my dress. That feels way too intimate. Plus, my aunt has a closet full of designer dresses, some that she's never even worn.

I'm sure I'll be able to find something.

"It will be fun," he murmurs softly as the waitress comes over with our food. Normally, I'd say he's lying. Getting dressed up is one of my least favorite things to do, but I enjoy spending time with him, so I'm actually looking forward to it.

Chapter 8

Brodie

With my hands full, I walk across my living room and back to the kitchen, where I left Reese filling a glass with ice for us and Jeb waiting to see if she accidentally drops some so he can eat it. The dog loves eating ice, maybe even more than the treats he begs for regularly. When I step around the corner, her eyes meet mine, and all I can think about is how pretty she is with her hair still windblown from us walking on the beach with Jeb after dinner and her nose slightly red from the sun before it set while we watched.

"Those are sports drinks?" She frowns at the plain black-labeled bottles I place on the island.

"Yeah. They haven't shared the packaging yet and don't want anyone snapping a picture and posting it online before they go public. Plus, one of the flavors is only supposed to be available for a limited time."

"So, this is a big deal."

"I guess in the world of sports drinks, it is."

"Cool." She hops up onto the counter to sit. "Which one first?"

I tip the bottle over and see the color of the liquid inside through the clear bottom. "How about red?"

"Red, it is." She holds up her glass, and I open the bottle, pouring some into it for her. She takes a sip and scrunches her nose.

"Bad?"

"It tastes salty, like all sports drinks do to me, but the flavor isn't bad. It's kind of like fruit punch." She hands the glass over to me, and I take a sip.

"It's not bad. And it doesn't taste like dirty bathwater." I watch her smile.

"Which one next?"

"You choose." She picks up the bottle in the middle and pours some of the bright green liquid into the glass. After she takes a sip, she holds the glass out to me, her expression blank. "Do you like it?"

"Just try it." I take a sip and gag.

"You're evil." I mock glare at her when she laughs. "What the fuck is this?" I smell the glass and almost gag again.

"It tastes like pickle juice." She takes the glass back and sips more. "I kind of like it."

"There's something wrong with you." I grab the glass and rinse it out. "Hopefully, that's the flavor they said is only available for a limited time."

"If it is, kids will love it, even if they only buy it to dare each other to drink it."

"True." I laugh while I get more ice and a few extra pieces for Jeb. After tossing them to him, I take the glass back to Ree. She opens another bottle and dumps some crystal blue liquid into the clear cup. When she reaches for it, I shake my head.

"You don't trust me?" She holds her hand over her heart.

"Not anymore." I raise the glass to my nose and smell it while she laughs. I take a sip when I don't smell anything odd. "Not bad." I hold the glass out to her, and she eyes me wearily. "What, you don't trust me?"

"Should I?"

"I'm not the one who didn't warn you about the pickle juice."

"It says a lot about someone when they can't let things go."

"It happened two minutes ago."

With a smile, she grips the glass and takes a drink. "Oh, I like this one." She drinks more.

I shake my head. "And here you thought I was trying to play you." I open the last bottle. When I pour out the liquid, it's bright yellow. After trying it, I pass the glass to her and watch her take a sip. Then, her eyes widen. Leaning over, she spits into the sink.

"What the heck is that?" She wipes her mouth with the back of her hand.

"My guess? Lemon."

"It tastes like Mr. Clean." She laughs, and I watch with my hands fisted at my sides so I don't do something stupid like reach for her, tangle my fingers in her hair, and kiss her.

Her eyes meet mine, and her hilarity dies instantly, like she knows what I'm thinking. Swallowing, her gaze drops to my mouth, and electricity seems to vibrate through the air between us. Without thinking, I take a step toward her and then curse under my breath when her cell phone rings, breaking into the moment.

Fuck.

Hopping off the counter, she goes to her bag, takes out her phone to check the screen, and then taps the side, sending whoever it was to voicemail. She looks up at me after shoving her cell back into her purse. "I should—"

"Do you want to watch a movie?" I cut her off before she can tell me that she should leave because I know that's what's coming.

"Um." She rubs her lips together, her gaze dropping to my mouth so quickly that I would've missed it if I weren't watching her so closely. "Sure, okay. Yeah."

I don't give her a chance to change her mind. I walk into the living room and take a seat on the couch. She doesn't sit next to me; she sits as far from me as she can get. I hide my smile and turn on the TV. After some bickering, we agree on the first *Saw* movie. As it begins, I feel her eyes on me more than once. I don't ask her what she's thinking. Instead, I decide to just let her work things out in her head. It's obvious there is something between us, but after finding out tonight at dinner that her ex cheated on her, I now understand why she has her guard up. The thing is, I'm not in a rush. I have all the time in the world to see where things go.

Chapter 9

Reese

"What about this one?" I hold one of Aunt Ileana's dresses in front of me so she can see me on the iPad I have propped up in her closet against her mirror.

"Boring," she calls out, and I roll my eyes. It's the third time she's yelled the same thing in the last ten minutes. As I assumed when I told her that Brodie invited me to go to New York with him for a fundraiser, the first words out of her mouth were, "Don't buy a dress until you look through my closet." Wait, that's a lie. The first words out of her mouth were, "I need to look into him before you accept his offer." Ten minutes after googling him with Marco at her side, she told me to raid her closet.

"What part of this dress is boring?" I ask, looking down at the sleeveless red dress with its high neckline, pretty lace, and sheer-panel details.

"It's not you. You're young and beautiful. That dress doesn't show enough skin."

"Should you be telling her she needs to show more skin?" Marco asks, looking at my aunt with a frown.

"She's going on a date with a handsome man; of course, she should show more skin."

"It's not a date," I cut in, and her gaze moves to me. "Brodie and I are just friends, remember?"

"Of course." I swear she rolls her eyes, but the iPad is so far away, I can't tell for sure. Shaking my head, I rehang the red dress and go back to sliding through her rack of dresses. When I notice a hanger with nothing on it, I begin to take it out just to hang it back with all her unused hangers. But when I tug it off the bar, I notice that it does have a dress on it, but the straps are so thin they're almost invisible against the black hanger, and the dress is cut so low I didn't see it before. My heart starts beating funny when I pull it fully out of its spot. The dress is absolutely beautiful. It's also very, very sexy. The top is a lace bustier with a sweetheart neckline and black velvet detailing outlining the cups that almost look like a built-in bra. The black lace over the sheer material is body-hugging and would likely hit me at about mid-calf.

"Try it on," I hear Aunt Ileana say and look across the closet. "I bought that twenty years ago in Paris and never had an occasion to wear it."

"It's so delicate." And it is. The lace material is so finely detailed that one snag could cause major damage.

"Try it on," she repeats. So, with a nod, I take it to her bathroom and close the door. It takes some effort to get myself into the dress and zip it up, but as soon as I have it on, I know it's the one. Not only do I feel beautiful, but it fits me perfectly. I poke my head out the door and shout, "Don't look yet."

"Okay," she calls back, and I rush across the room to her heels and grab a pair of strappy, flesh-colored sandals off her shelf. They have a high heel and a thin strap that crosses over the tops of my toes and then wraps around my ankle. When they're on, I tie my hair back into a slicked-back ponytail and walk toward my iPad.

"Ready," I say, and my aunt's face appears on the screen.

"Oh, my beautiful girl." She covers her mouth with her hand. "It's…"

"Perfect," Marco finishes for her softly.

"Yes. It's perfect." She smiles at me. "That dress looks beautiful on you, Reese."

"Are you sure you're okay with me borrowing it?"

"It's yours. It was obviously made for you." She smiles and then glances at my feet, grinning. "The shoes, on the other hand, you'll have to return."

Laughing, I turn to my side and take myself in. With the sun I've been getting, my skin isn't its normal pale shade but a golden-bronze.

And my hair has lightened in places, making it seem almost as if I had highlights put in. I don't look like the same woman who moved here a couple of months ago. And I don't feel like her either. I'm happy—happier than I've been in years.

"What are your plans this evening?" Marco asks as I take off the heels.

"Brodie said he got the stuff to make kitchen sink cookies, so we are doing that and watching a movie."

"You two have been spending a lot of time together," Aunt Ileana says casually, but I know her. And I know there was nothing casual about that comment. She's digging, hoping I'll tell her that something is going on between us. *Like that I'm pretty sure he was going to kiss me yesterday evening. And I'm also pretty sure I would have kissed him back.*

"We're friends. And as he explained to me, this is his time off. When he starts practicing soon, I probably won't see him as much."

"He told you that he won't see you as much?"

I frown. "No, he just told me he will have to practice most days."

"Hmm." She hums, and I shake my head at her. "I'm going to go change and then head up to his place. I love you."

"Love you, too. Have fun tonight."

"Thank you. And thanks again for letting me raid your closet."

"What's mine is yours." She smiles. "I'll call you when we get to Rome since we are traveling tomorrow."

"Okay, be safe." I blow her and Marco a kiss and then wander back into the bathroom, carefully getting out of the dress. When it's back on the hanger, I put on the sweats and tank top I had been wearing earlier, then check on Mickey to make sure he's good before leaving the apartment and taking the elevator up to the penthouse on the top floor.

When I get to Brodie's door, I knock and wait, then knock again when he doesn't answer after a couple of minutes. Taking out my cell, I check the time. I'm a few minutes early, but only a few. He should be here. The door swings inward, startling me, and my head flies up. I blink as my eyes collide with a half-naked Brodie wearing nothing but a thick white towel around his waist, his broad chest beaded with water. I swallow while my nipples pebble and the space between my legs throbs. You'd think, having seen him in swim trunks, I would be able to control my reaction to seeing him like he is now—or mostly like he is now because I've never seen him dripping wet, and his towel is doing nothing to hide just how well-endowed he is.

"Sorry, my agent called when I was just finishing with my workout, and I didn't realize what time it was, so I jumped in the shower." He reaches for my hand and drags me into his apartment, which is a good thing because I doubt I could have gotten my feet to move on their own.

"No problem." I look anywhere but at him, then thank my lucky stars when Jeb decides to make an appearance at that moment and comes to greet me. "You can get dressed." It sounds like an order, and he laughs.

I glance up at him while I rub Jeb's head. Yep, he's laughing, or he was. Now, he's just smiling at me like he thinks I'm funny. My cheeks warm. "I'll be right back. The stuff for the cookies is on the counter with the recipe."

He turns and starts down the hall, and I watch the muscles in his back move as he disappears out of sight. Looking down at Jeb, I drag in a breath and then wander to the kitchen. Because Brodie isn't here to tell me I can't, I give Jeb a couple of treats from his jar, then pick up the cookie recipe. I've never heard of kitchen sink cookies before, but as I look over the ingredients, I know they will be delicious. They have butterscotch chips, both dark chocolate and regular chocolate chips, pretzels, toffy bits, and coarse sea salt. They sound sweet and salty—my favorite combo.

"Ready?" I look up at Brodie when he walks around the edge of the counter and groan inwardly because while he did get dressed, he forgot a shirt. And since he's a guy, he doesn't technically need one.

"Is it safe to bake without a shirt on?" The question is out before I can stop it, and he grins, rubbing his hands over his ridged stomach.

"We're not frying anything, so I think I'll be okay."

"Right," I mumble, disappointed.

Walking to where I'm standing, I hold my breath when his big body presses into mine, and he reaches around me for the standing mixer on the counter.

"How was work?" he asks, plugging it in.

"Umm. Good. Busy." I bite my bottom lip when he moves into my space again and starts opening the bags on the counter.

"I got our plane tickets. Our flight is at almost eight, so that should give you plenty of time to come home and get ready before we head to the airport."

"Great." I step to the side to give him some room—or me some room. Grabbing the butter, I open two sticks and put them in the mixing bowl while he starts measuring the sugar.

"My shoot is at seven a.m. on Saturday, so I figure you can sleep in while I take care of that. Then we can go have breakfast and explore the city. I know you said you've been to New York, but is there anywhere you want to go?"

"The library." I glance over at him. "I haven't ever gone to the New York City Library, and I know I can't take any books out, but I'd like to see it in person."

His smile is soft. "I can make that happen."

"Thanks." I smile back, and then the two of us work in sync, making cookies that are just as delicious as I imagined they would be. The movie we decided to watch, however, is absolutely horrible. But in the end, it doesn't matter because everything seems a little better when I'm with Brodie.

Chapter 10

Reese

Picking my Red Bull off the bathroom counter in my hotel room, I yawn and then take another drink. I'm already exhausted and have at least another six hours before I can sleep.

Last night, Brodie and I got into New York late. By the time we got to the hotel downtown and checked in, it was after midnight, and we were both starving. Thankfully, we were in a city that never sleeps, so we could walk down the block for a slice of pizza. Then, because at that point I was wired, we walked to Times Square to see the lights. By the time I climbed into bed, it was almost two in the morning, and then I woke up at ten to Brodie knocking on the door. He had been up early for his shoot and looked bright-eyed and bushy-tailed, despite getting less sleep than I did. While I got ready and drank the coffee he'd brought, he lounged on my bed, talking to me through the open bathroom door. Then, the two of us wandered the city together.

We went to a cute little café for breakfast, the New York City Library, which was so cool to see in person, the *Ghostbusters* firehouse, and the abandoned Track 61. After all that, we wandered through Central Park, where we each ate a hotdog while lounging on the grass. The day was magical. Then again, being with Brodie anywhere was its own kind of magic.

With another yawn, I grab my makeup bag and start the process of getting myself ready. I never wear much makeup, and that is not changing tonight, but I did get talked into buying red lipstick the same day I bought myself my own pair of strappy heels from Neiman Marcus. I'll wear it tonight like the girl at the makeup counter taught me.

With my hair tied back away from my face in a tight ponytail that I took extra time making look perfect—even wrapping an under piece around the hair tie and securing it with a bobby pin—I add bronzer to my face, some blush, a little gel to my brows so they stay in place, and then line my lips and add the lipstick that is supposed to stay put for twenty-four hours.

When I'm finished and lean back to look at myself in the mirror, I blink at my reflection. I look like my aunt. I never noticed it before, maybe because I never wear makeup, but I look just like her, which means I look just like my dad. The realization makes me feel oddly connected to him.

Knowing Brodie will arrive any minute so we can get to the hotel where the event is being held, I finish up in the bathroom and then get dressed.

When I have my shoes on, I grab the small clutch I borrowed from my aunt and start adding things to it—not much. My ID, a little cash, my phone, the lipstick just in case, and... I look at the door that separates Brodie's room from mine when I hear a knock.

Wandering to it, I open it and swallow. I should have known that Brodie in a tuxedo would be hard to handle. Heck, him wearing the shorts and tee he'd had on this afternoon made it difficult to focus. Then again, his shirt fit him like a second skin, and knowing what was under it had me imagining it off more than once. But in a tux? In a tux, he looks like he should be on a red carpet somewhere with some pretty little supermodel on his arm.

"Jesus Christ, Ree." Snapping out of my runaway thoughts, I lift my gaze to his, and the world feels like it shifts under my feet when I see the look in his eyes. "You look..." He takes a step toward me, and I hold my ground. "You look beautiful." His eyes wander slowly down my dress to my heels. "I didn't think you could look any more beautiful than you do every single day, but you proved me wrong." Oh, God. My heart is going to pound out of my chest. Either that, or I'm going to faint. "That dress." I swear I hear him growl or groan and see his hands fist at his sides. "It's perfect. You look perfect."

"Thank you," I finally get out, and his heated gaze meets mine.

Kiss me. The thought slams into my head so hard it catches me off guard. But I want it. I want him to kiss me. Like he knows exactly what I'm thinking, he takes another step toward me and wraps his large palm around my hip. His other hand goes to the side of my throat, then with his thumb on my chin, his lips lower to my...cheek. My eyes slide closed in disappointment. When I open them, his face is an inch from mine.

"Are you ready?"

So close. He's *so close* I could kiss him if I were brave enough to just press my mouth to his. Am I? Could I do it? Should I? I like him a lot, and I like the easy connection we have. I like being his friend. But some part of me wants more. I don't know when I decided that, but it's true. I want more from him.

"Ree." His thumb runs along my jaw, and I drop my gaze to his mouth. "Fuck," he groans. I don't know where I find the courage, but I lift onto my toes and press my mouth to his.

Just like that, something breaks between us, and whatever he had been using to hold himself back snaps. He doesn't kiss me back; he completely takes over the kiss, holding my jaw, tilting my head, and touching his tongue to my bottom lip. I open for him instinctively and follow his lead. My heart pounds, my skin feels tight, and every part of me presses closer to him, wanting more. I've never experienced this kind of moment, and I feel greedy. Greedy and desperate for more. If my dress weren't so tight, I would attempt to climb him, try to wrap my legs around his waist to get closer to the hard length of him pressing into my belly. When he nips my bottom lip and palms my ass, I whimper in need.

"Christ." He licks into my mouth, then his lips and teeth join in, and his tongue works its way down my throat.

"Oh, God." My head falls back when he nips the top of my breast.

"Fuck, Ree."

"Please, touch me," I beg, and he groans as my nails dig into his scalp.

"I will, but not now." He kisses me again, deep and wet, before slowing the kiss and pulling away, breathing heavily. "The car is waiting for us downstairs." He presses one more kiss to my lips, and my lashes flutter open. Damn... Right. I forgot we were supposed to be leaving, not making out in my hotel room.

"I fucking love that you look disappointed." He smiles, running his thumb under my bottom lip. "And I fucking hate that we have to leave." He swipes his thumb under my bottom lip once more. "Are you ready?"

"I just..." I lick my lips, which now taste like him and mint. "I just need to check and make sure my makeup is okay."

"You look perfect, but I'll wait." He seems reluctant to let me go but does it anyway. While he waits, I walk into the bathroom and make sure my lipstick is still in place. By some miracle it is, which is a testament to the quality, and probably why it costs sixty dollars. I do, however, have to fix my hair. So, I do that and then walk back into the room, picking up my bag from the bed to finish putting my stuff inside. When I'm done, I meet him at the door, and he takes my hand, threading his fingers through mine. He doesn't let it go until he has to so we can both get into the car waiting for us.

Chapter 11

Brodie

I've been around beautiful women my entire career. I've fucked them, had them use me, and used them, too. I've fallen in love with them, and was loved back more than once, but I've never felt prouder than I do when I take Reese's hand and help her out of the car. It's not because she looks absolutely stunning—although, she does—it's just her. Her brain, her ability to make me laugh, and how fucking happy I am just being in her presence. As soon as she's got both feet on the pavement, and before we even reach the red carpet leading into the hotel, cameras begin going off, startling her. Wrapping my arm around her waist, I smile and wave when my name is called, but I don't stop to talk to the press.

"I think you forgot to tell me about the camera thing," she whispers, leaning into me when we get inside. I look down at her.

"Sorry. I should have thought about it. I'm just so used to it."

"It's okay, I was just caught off guard." She takes her eyes off mine and looks around, then her eyes widen. "Is that the famous basketball player who is in all those Papa John's pizza commercials?"

"Probably." I don't bother taking my eyes off her to look over and confirm. "There are lots of players from all different sports here tonight." She looks up at me. "This event helps raise money for youth sports in big cities that don't get the funding they need for gear and travel expenses."

"That's cool."

"Do you want to walk around and see what's up for auction?"

"Sure." She takes my hand, and the two of us walk into the ballroom, where tables are lined up with different items up for grabs, from sports memorabilia to an entire island available for a week, including a chef and staff. As she looks at a pair of earrings, I turn my head when I feel eyes on us, and frown at the guy standing a few feet away staring at Reese in a familiar way that sets my teeth on edge. He's tall with broad shoulders and looks familiar, but I can't place him. Resting my hand on Ree's lower back, I watch his eyes travel from my hand up to my arm. When his gaze meets mine, he looks shocked. *What the fuck is that about?*

"Ree."

"Yeah?" She tips her head back, and I bend my neck to whisper in her ear.

"Do you know that guy?"

She pulls back to look me in the eye, then, with her brows together, glances around. I feel her muscles under my palm bunch when her eyes land on the guy still staring.

"Shit," she whispers, turning toward me and bumping into my chest.

"Shit, what?" I ask as she steps around me, grabs my hand, and starts dragging me away in the opposite direction of the guy.

"That's my best friend, Kirk. Or he *was* my best friend."

I frown, and she glances up at me, rolling her eyes.

"My ex-boyfriend?"

"The one that fucked your sister?" I stop allowing her to pull me along, and she comes to a halt with me.

"She's not my sister. She's my mom's fiancé's daughter. But...yes."

"Why the fuck is he here?"

"I don't know. I haven't talked to him. But he did just sign with one of the NFL teams here in New York, so he might be here for the same reason you are."

I blink at her. "He plays for the NFL?" I glance over my shoulder at him. Shit, now I know why he looks familiar. Kirk Finer is not just a football player; he's one of the NFL's top draft picks this year. And he used to date my girl.

"Does it matter that he plays for the NFL?" No, but also...fuck yeah. I'd thought her ex would... Well, honestly, I assumed he would look like one of the dudes who used to get straight As in science class back in college. I didn't know he was Kirk Finer. I look over her head and see him walking our way. "He's coming over here."

"Great." She groans, and I almost laugh.

"It's fine, just play it cool."

"Uh, Reese?" he says, his tone unsure as he stops a foot from us.

Her shoulders fall, and her forehead drops to my chest. Then, after a deep breath, she tips her head back and glares at me like this is my fault before spinning around.

"Kirk." There is no warmth in the greeting.

"I thought that was you. Then I wasn't sure because..." He glances up at me quickly before refocusing on her. "Wow, you look amazing." He lets his eyes wander over her and her dress, and I want to punch him in his fucking face so fucking bad. Instead, I wrap my arm around her and tuck her snugly against my side.

"You are?" I ask, playing stupid. He pulls his eyes off her to meet my gaze.

"Kirk Finer. And you're Brodie Larsen. I used to watch you when you played for Tennessee."

"How do you know my girlfriend?" I ask, again playing stupid but also wanting him to know she's mine. And yes, she *is* mine, and I don't give a fuck that we've only shared one kiss or haven't talked about where this is going. I'm claiming her. We'll figure out the rest with time.

"We were..."

"What we were doesn't matter." She cuts him off, and hurt fills his eyes as he looks at her.

"I've tried to call and text."

"Sorry, I've been busy."

"Kirk." A blonde in a tight red dress walks up to join us, and I feel Ree's spine stiffen as the female who looks like every sorority girl I've ever known slides her arm through Kirk's. "I've been looking for you." She smiles up at him and then looks at us, her plastic smile firmly in place before her gaze lands on Ree.

"Reese?" Her smile slides away, and her eyes widen.

Shit, this must be the stepsister.

"I..." Kirk glances at whatever her name is and then looks at Reese, remorse slashing through his features. "Can we talk?" He glances at me quickly, while Ree's nails dig into my side through my tux. "Alone? Just for a few minutes."

"Sorry," I cut in before Ree can respond, then look down at her. "We need to go find our table, baby."

"Of course." She leans her weight into me and then looks at Kirk. "Have a good night, Kirk." Then she dips her chin toward the woman on his arm. "Melissa." Turning her away from the two of them, I start walking her through the room, then lean down and whisper, "Are you okay?"

"I don't know. I wasn't expecting to see him, and I really wasn't expecting to see *her*, so I just…" She glances up at me. "I don't know what I feel right now besides blindsided."

"That's understandable." I squeeze her hip, and she returns the gesture by squeezing my waist.

"Thank you for rescuing me again."

"I didn't rescue you."

"You did by not giving him the opportunity to talk to me alone."

"That wasn't me rescuing you, Ree. That was me being selfish and territorial," I mutter honestly, stopping at the board where the table assignments are laid out.

"Well, still. Thank you." She presses her body into mine. "Where are we sitting? And please don't tell me we're sitting with them."

"You're safe." I point at the list of people at the table with us. "Do you want a drink before we go over?"

"Yes. Tequila. I've never had it, but I've heard it's the go-to drink when you want to wake up the next day with no memory of the night before."

"How about a glass of wine since I'd like you to remember tonight?" I laugh and lean down, touching my mouth to hers without thinking. She kisses me back with ease.

Chapter 12

Reese

Picking up my drink, I take a sip while listening to the woman seated next to me talk about her husband, who is not here tonight because he has a soccer match in London tomorrow. From what I've gathered, he's world-renowned, yet I have no idea who he is. Not that that means much of anything. There must be over two hundred famous men and women in this room right now, and even though a few of them look familiar, I don't know any of their names.

Which is sad. I could probably make a killing if I stole a stack of napkins and walked around asking for autographs to sell on eBay.

"I love your dress. Where did you get it?" she asks, and I place my glass of wine on the table. I really should have gotten tequila.

"My aunt got it in Paris twenty years ago."

"Oh, I love vintage. It's beautiful." She leans back from the table to expose more of her dress, and I take that as my cue to return the compliment.

God, I really do suck at this.

"I love your dress, too. That color is really nice. It reminds me of a flamingo."

"A flamingo?" She frowns.

"The pink bird."

"I know what a flamingo is."

"Oh, sorry, I just..."

"Ree," Brodie cuts in before I can shove my foot farther into my mouth. "Do you want to dance?"

No. "Yes, please." I let out a relieved breath and then glance at the woman again. I really should have asked for her name. We just finished a whole meal together, sitting side by side. "We'll be right back. We're just going for a spin."

"Sure." She nods, looking at me like I have two heads. I take Brodie's hand and let him help me out of my chair. With one look at his handsome face, I know he's trying not to laugh.

When we get to the dance floor, he pulls my body into his and drops his mouth to my ear.

"Did you just tell Ronaldo's wife that she looks like a flamingo?"

"No. I said her dress reminded me of a flamingo," I grumble, and he laughs. "It's pink. What else was I supposed to say?"

"Nothing." He smiles down at me, looking amused.

"Do you like this kind of thing?" I look around at the people chatting in groups and others dancing near us. It's a lot to take in, and I don't know that I could do this on a regular basis.

"What? Events like this?" I nod. "I don't know if I *like* them, but it's a good way to meet other athletes and build connections. Plus, this is all for a good cause. My family could afford to pay for my gear and shit when I started playing hockey, but that isn't the case for everyone." His gaze wanders over my face. "Why do you ask?"

"I'm just not good at this. I've never been overly social, so I feel really outside my comfort zone, which I know makes me extra awkward. Hence me telling that nice woman her dress looks like a flamingo." I watch him smile and melt into him. "Plus, I don't recognize anyone and feel like I should when I'm in a room full of famous people."

"Who cares if you don't know who any of these people are? If you started talking about one of the sea creatures from your science-y books, I doubt any of us in this room would know what you're talking about."

"Science-y books?" I grin, but he doesn't smile back. The look on his face is deathly serious.

"You're perfect, Ree, and fuck anyone who doesn't think so." He dips his face closer to mine. "And I knew it before, but I hope you get that your ex is the world's biggest fucking idiot. I know it sucks because he hurt you, but I gotta tell you, Ree, I'm half-tempted to send him a thank you gift for fucking up because if he hadn't, I don't know that we would have met. And I'm really fucking happy we did."

"Are you trying to make me cry?"

"Do not start crying. I don't think I could handle seeing you cry," he grumbles, and I drop my forehead to the center of his chest, attempting to pull myself together because my nose is actually starting to sting.

"You do know that you're pretty awesome, too, right?" I say quietly, lifting my gaze back to his. "I'm also really glad that things worked out like they did and that we met."

His expression softens, and my heart pounds as he presses his mouth to mine for a soft kiss. Shit, I'm falling for him—or I think I am. I have never felt like this about another man, and all of this is so new to me. When he pulls back, he touches my jaw softly and then looks over my head when someone calls his name.

"Fuck."

"Do I even want to know?"

"It's just my agent." He laughs, giving my waist a squeeze.

"Oh, okay. Well, while you go talk to him, I'm going to use the restroom."

"Come back to me when you're done." I nod and step out of his embrace, heading to the restroom while he walks toward a very short man with almost no hair on the top of his head.

After I finish in the bathroom, I step out into the hall and silently curse when I see Kirk standing there, leaning against the wall with his head back and his eyes closed.

I start to sneak past him, hoping he won't notice me, but my plan is thwarted when he opens his eyes, and they lock on mine.

Great.

"Reese." He pushes away from the wall and steps in front of me.

"Sorry, I can't talk. Brodie is waiting for me."

"Please." He holds his hands up in front of him. "I just want to talk to you for a minute."

Since he's blocking the hall, and I don't want to cause a scene, I cross my arms over my chest. "Fine. Say what you want to say."

"I'm sorry. I never planned on anything happening between Melissa and me, but you and I were in an awkward place, and we hadn't..." He glances behind me and shuts his mouth.

"Had sex," I finish for him. His gaze comes back to mine. "So, because I hadn't had sex with you, you decided to sleep with Melissa?"

"It wasn't that..." He scrubs his fingers through his hair. "Or it was partly that, but…"

"But what?" I swear I want to kick him in the shin. When I agreed to be his girlfriend, nothing between us changed except the intimacy part of our relationship. But even that only went so far. I mean, we were working up to it, but it was all very uncomfortable for me. So, we hadn't had sex. He thought it was because I was still a virgin, and I convinced myself of the same thing. Now, I realize it was because he was Kirk, my best friend, the guy I grew up with. We knew everything about each other, and I loved him, but I just wasn't attracted to him like that. I never had the urge to crawl up his body. I never wanted to kiss him or have him kiss me. There was no desire on my end, and that should have been my first clue that I should have broken up with him. Did he feel the same? Probably. Or maybe. Who knew?

"But I shouldn't have asked you to be my girlfriend." He takes a step toward me, and I back up into something—or someone. Then a hand wraps around my hip in a familiar way, and I know without looking that it's Brodie. Great, how long was he standing there? "We were getting ready to graduate, and I was scared that I would lose you. Part of me thought we could make it work."

"You know all of this could have been avoided if you had just been honest with me. I don't care that you're with her, and sure, no guy wants to tell their girlfriend they're falling for someone else, but before the dynamic of our relationship changed, you and I were best friends. That should have trumped everything else."

"You're right."

"And you should have known me well enough to know that I would have been okay with you dating Melissa if that's what you wanted, even if I don't like her very much."

"I fucked up."

"You did, but so did I. I shouldn't have agreed to be with you either. I knew it wouldn't work, but like you, I didn't want to lose you and thought agreeing to be your girlfriend was the only way to keep you in my life."

"I'm sorry."

"Me, too." My smile is sad because I know that even with this conversation, there is no going back to us being friends.

"Can you forgive me?"

"Yes, but that doesn't mean we can go back to being friends like we were."

"I get that. I don't like it, but I get it," he says quietly, then looks at the man behind me, his eyes narrowing the way they used to do when we were kids, and someone was picking on me. "You'd better be good to her." I sigh and barely avoid rolling my eyes at him when his gaze meets mine once again. "Take care, Reese."

"You, too." I watch him walk off. When he's out of sight, I turn to face Brodie. "How much of that conversation did you hear?"

"I walked out of the bathroom when he said that you and he were in an awkward place."

So, basically everything. "Great." I let out a breath. "Well, now you know that I've never had sex, so that's fun."

He drops his chin and locks his eyes on mine. "You mean you never had sex with him."

"Umm," I whisper, caught off guard when he suddenly begins walking me backward. My back hits the wall, and then he cages me in with his big body.

"Are you a virgin, Ree?" he asks on a growl that sends a tingle down my spine.

"Why are you saying it like that?" Also, why is my heart pounding and the space between my legs suddenly pulsing?

"Answer my question."

"Maybe." My breath catches as his hand smooths up the side of my waist, coming to rest just below my breast.

"Has anyone ever been inside you?"

"Brodie."

"Yes? Or no?"

"No."

"Shit." He drops his head to my shoulder.

"Shit, what?" I ask, worry beginning to creep up on me. I know there were guys back in college who would refuse to sleep with a girl if she was a virgin because they didn't want to risk the attachment. Pulling back, Brodie's eyes meet mine, and then he presses his hips into my belly.

"I'm hard as steel, and there is a room full of people down the hall, Ree."

"Oh."

"Yeah, oh."

I lick my lips. "It doesn't bother you that...?"

"That you're a virgin?" I nod. "Fuck, no." His eyes wander over my face for a long moment, and then he takes a step back, not fully out of my space but far enough away that I can no longer feel his erection. I watch him adjust himself and bite my bottom lip. "Don't look at me like that, Ree. We still have at least another hour here."

"Okay," I breathe, and his jaw clenches. I press my palms flat against the wall behind me so I don't reach for him like I want to. Have I ever felt this desirable, this powerful? No, I don't think I have. I've also never been this turned on, so the next hour will be interesting.

Chapter 13

Brodie

With my hand wrapped around Ree's thigh, I watch the city lights go by and attempt to get myself under control. This evening was a test of my willpower, and if I could have left the fundraiser an hour ago, I would have. But I knew there was no way I'd be able to get away without Doug calling me out for my early departure.

When the car pulls up outside the hotel, I push the door open and then reach in to take Ree's hand, helping her out. Once she's on her feet outside the car, I lean in and thank the driver before slamming the door closed. Taking her hand in mine, I walk with her into the hotel and lead her to the elevator. Neither of us has said a word since we left the fundraiser, but there has been an undercurrent of sexual tension building since I had her pressed up against that wall in the hall at the event. The elevator doors open, and we both step on. I press the button for our floor and look down, finding her fidgeting with her clutch like she's nervous.

Her eyes lift to mine, dark and heated with desire, her cheeks slightly pink. No, she's not nervous; she's turned on. And I haven't even touched her yet. My hands fist at my sides. *Virgin. She's a virgin.* The knowledge makes me want her more, but it also reminds me that I need to take this slowly, even if it kills me.

The doors open on our floor, and I somehow manage not to pick her up and carry her down the hall to my room. I also somehow manage to get out my key card to open the door without fumbling. As soon as the door closes behind us, she turns to face me, and the live wire set to ignite all evening goes off with a bang. The two of us lunge in a blur of hands, mouths, and teeth as we go at each other with abandon. I get off my jacket, then get distracted by the noises she makes as I nip her collarbone. While she works on the buttons of my shirt, I unzip the back of her dress and kiss down her shoulder, then grin when she makes a disgruntled sound. Capturing her mouth with mine, I take over for her with the buttons and shrug off my shirt while her dress pools around her waist, exposing the strapless lace bra she's wearing. I lose her mouth for a moment when I toss my shirt away and help her out of her dress, adding it to the pile of clothes on the chair in the corner. Afterward, I walk her backward to the bed. When she falls against the mattress onto her back, I loom over her, taking her mouth again and sliding my hands behind her back to unhook her bra before kissing down her chest and pulling it out from under her, tossing it away. Lifting my head as I stand, I take in her exposed breasts and pretty pink nipples, then run my hand down the top of her thigh around to her calf and lift her ankle. Her shoes are just as sexy as her dress, and it takes me a minute to unclasp them. Once I have both off, I take out my wallet and toss it onto the bed, then put one knee on the mattress and settle between her legs.

"Brodie," she breathes against my mouth, lifting her hips into mine as I move my hand up her inner thigh. "You have too many clothes on."

"I do. But I also want to make this good for you, and if I take off my pants, I won't be able to slow down." I kiss her, my hand moving farther up her thigh. Then my fingers skim over the lace covering her, and I bite back a curse. She's soaking wet. I move the material aside and slip my fingers through her wet folds, rolling the tips over her clit. She whimpers and lifts her hips.

"You're so wet, Ree," I groan, circling her clit and causing her hips to buck.

"Oh, God," she moans when I lean down and pull one of her breasts into my mouth. Her nipple hardens against my tongue, and her fingers dig into my scalp. I move to her other breast to do the same. "Please," she begs. Knowing what she wants, my fingers glide down farther, and then I slide my middle finger inside her, her walls clamping down on it like a vise. She's so tight, so damn perfect. I enter her with another finger and take her mouth again while using my thumb on her clit. When her pussy begins to pulse, I pull back and watch her, listening to her breath hitch as she comes on my hand.

When I know the waves of her orgasm have passed, I slide my fingers out of her and stand, then quickly lose the rest of my clothes. Her eyes open to half-mast and meet mine when I pull the lace of her underwear down her hips. She lifts her bottom to help. I toss them away, and she sits up when I kneel on the bed with my hand wrapped around my cock, throbbing in sync with my heartbeat.

"Umm." She licks her lips, lifting her heated eyes to mine. "I think this is where I ask you if that's going to fit."

I laugh. Jesus. She's the only woman I've ever known who joked during sex. "We'll make it work." I walk on my knees farther onto the bed, then fall to my ass with my back against the headboard.

"Come here, Ree." I hold out my hand, and she takes it, looking nervous for the first time this evening. Once I have her adjusted on my lap, I cup her breast that fits my palm perfectly, then move one hand to the back of her neck to drag her mouth down to mine. When she's back to being turned on, and her body is relaxed against mine, I let her mouth go and reach for my wallet, taking out a condom. She watches, fascinated as I roll it down the length of my dick. Once it's in place, I tip my head back to her. "You're in charge." I grab her ass and pull her pussy closer to my cock, then lift her until I'm poised at her entrance. She whimpers, grabbing my shoulders with her eyes locked on mine. "Take as much of me as you can handle, Ree."

Biting her bottom lip, she begins to lower herself onto my length, and it takes all my willpower not to slam her down onto my lap as she moves torturously slow. Gritting my teeth, I hold on to her hips as I watch myself disappear inside of her. Fuck. I can't do that. I'm going to come if I watch, so I distract myself with her breasts bobbing in front of my face. I lean forward and pull one of them into my mouth. When I do, she jerks, and her inner walls contract. She also takes more of me. I let that breast go and do the same with the other, getting the same reaction. When she moans, and her nails dig into my shoulders, I look up to make sure she's okay. Her head is back, her eyes closed, lips swollen, and cheeks pink. She lifts onto her knees and then sinks down more on my length. Goddamn, she's tight. So fucking tight and wet, it's killing me not to fuck her. But if I die now, I'll go happily.

"Brodie." My name leaves her mouth on a whimper when she's fully seated on my lap. I let her breast go and wrap my hand around the back of her neck. Her mouth lands on mine, and as I thrust my tongue between her lips, her hips rotate like she's attempting to get used to my size before lifting slightly and sliding back down. As she begins to settle into a slow rhythm, I move my hand between her legs. The noise she makes when I make contact with her clit causes my balls to draw up tight. Not wanting to come and knowing that is exactly what will happen if I don't get us in a different position, I sit forward, wrap my arms around her, and maneuver her to her back. The moment I'm settled between her thighs, she hooks her legs around my waist, and I instantly regret putting her under me. I have imagined her like this a million different times, but the reality is better than anything I ever came up with in my head. Her hair on my pillow, her warm, soft body under mine, the heat of her wrapped so snugly around my cock, and the expression on her face as she looks into my eyes. It all just about has me coming undone at the seams.

Sliding out of her and then back in, I grit my teeth and remind myself to go slow when every instinct I have is telling me to fuck her. Resting my fists against the mattress, I fall into a rhythm but the heels of her feet are soon urging me to go faster, pulling me in deeper on each downstroke. When her walls start tightening around my cock, I move my hand between us and barely touch her before she gasps, calling my name and digging her nails into my biceps as she comes. With a few more strokes, I follow her over the edge, no longer able to hold back. I lose myself inside of her with one last thrust of my hips.

Breathing heavily, I drop my forehead to her shoulder. She wraps herself around me, holding on tight.

After a couple of minutes, when I can talk myself into moving, I roll to my back, taking her with me. I lose her heat but gain her weight as she falls against my chest. Smiling to myself, I let my hands roam over her smooth skin and listen to her breathing even out as my heartbeat slows to a normal tempo.

"You okay?" I ask after a moment. She lifts her head, her eyes meeting mine, and then she flashes me a cute little smile.

"Yes. I'm just trying to figure out how this happened."

"Which part?"

"All of it." She laughs, placing her hands on my chest and then resting her chin on top of them. "One minute, you're the guy rescuing me from a dirtbag at the pool, and I've convinced myself we're going to be nothing more than friends. And now, I'm naked on top of you in a hotel room in New York City after we just had sex." She shakes her head. "It's a lot to wrap my mind around."

"Do you have any regrets?"

"No." She tips her head to the side. "Do you?"

"Fuck, no." I smooth my fingers up her spine.

"What now? What happens after this?"

"We go back to Florida and do the same thing we've been doing, only with a lot more of this included." I pat her bottom.

"So, this isn't a one-time thing?"

"No." The word comes out harsher than intended. "I know this is a lot to take in, but I like you. I like being with you and want to see where this goes. And I know you've got school, and I'll have training and away games, but I'm willing to put in the effort if you are."

"I'm willing to try," she says softly. I thread my fingers through her hair and then lean up to press my mouth to hers. When I pull back, I let my eyes wander over her pretty face for a long moment before sitting up with her and carrying her into the bathroom.

Chapter 14

Reese

Lying next to the pool on my belly with my eyes closed, I relish the feel of the sun on my skin and roll my eyes when Brodie's hand lands on my ass in a silent claim. He'd lied when we were in New York. Things *did* change when we got back to Florida but in the best possible ways. Not only the sex—I mean, that's at the top of the list—but his possessiveness is the thing I hadn't expected from him. And although I'm sure it makes me sound crazy, I like that he feels so territorial around me. It makes me feel oddly secure in our relationship and gives me a sense of power because I know I'm just as important to him as he is to me. Only time will tell how the two of us cope when his official season starts, and I begin school, but I have a feeling we'll figure it out just like we are now.

"What time is your aunt's flight getting in?" he asks, patting my bottom. I turn my head his way.

"Four. I told her and Marco that we'd have dinner with them tonight so they can meet you."

"Are we cooking or ordering in?"

"Ordering in." I lean up on my elbows so I can reach under my lounger and get my phone to check the time. "It's three. By the time they get out of the airport and home, it will be close to six."

"Enough time to shower." The smirk on his face causes my toes to curl. I like showering with him. I like lying in bed with him. I like being in the kitchen with him and…

"Ree, I can't see your eyes, yet I still know what you're thinking.

Stop, or I'm going to drag you upstairs. You're the one who wanted to come down to the pool."

"It's getting too hot to stay out anyway," I mutter, and he laughs. God, I love making him laugh. Or maybe it's just that I love him.

"Did you call your mom back?"

"Yes." I sigh, rolling to my back. "She and Richard decided they're going to have their wedding in Minnesota. That way, I can make it even if I have school."

"They want you there."

"I know."

"I'll be there with you."

"Like you have a choice." I look down at his hand when it lands on my thigh. Two days after New York, he convinced me to call my mom and tell her everything that'd happened between Kirk and me and exactly why I left Minnesota the way I did. It wasn't a comfortable conversation, especially when she put me on speaker so Richard could hear what I was saying. But I felt better afterward. And I felt validated when the two of them told me they understood why I left and said they didn't blame me for needing to get away. They did, however, make me feel guilty when they said they wished I would have told them everything from the beginning. Apparently, they'd thought they had done something wrong.

The day after I spoke with the two of them, Richard called me on his own to apologize on Melissa's behalf, then told me that if I ever come to visit my mom, regardless of Melissa being his daughter, he will make whatever arrangements are necessary so I don't ever feel uncomfortable in their home. It was sweet and made me like him a whole lot more.

"Are you ready to go back upstairs?" Brodie asks, cutting into my thoughts. I turn my head his way. I can't see his eyes with his sunglasses on, but I can feel his hot gaze on me.

"I think I want to stay down here for a while longer." I lift my arms above my head and hide my smile when he stands.

"Ree." He looms over me, his hand going to my thigh, his fingers digging in and making me squirm. "It's time to go upstairs."

I want to tease him and tell him no, but then his fingers slide farther up my inner thigh, and I know there is no way I'll be able to play that kind of game with him. He'll win every time without even trying.

"Okay." I bite my bottom lip and sit up. A few minutes later, we are both standing in the chilled elevator on the way up to his place, the moment feeling a little like it did all those weeks ago. Only now, things between us are totally different. I have never felt more comfortable just being myself with anyone. He accepts me just the way I am, and I return the favor, which isn't hard to do since he's pretty perfect.

"I love you," I blurt. He drops his gaze to mine. "I don't know how long you're supposed to wait to say that, but I do."

"Ree." He shakes his head while staring at me.

"Don't feel like you have to say it back," I say before he can tell me that he doesn't feel the same. "I just want you to know because… Well, because I do." I shake my head. "Love you, that is. And—" My babbling ends with a gasp when he wraps his hand around the back of my neck and pulls me forward, crashing his mouth down onto mine. The kiss is deep and wet, and so filled with emotion that I feel my nose sting. When he releases my mouth, he doesn't let me go. Instead, he drops his forehead to mine.

"I love you, too, Ree. So fucking much."

My heart swells with relief. "Good," I whisper, and he laughs.

"How did I get so lucky?"

"I don't know. I'm still trying to figure out how *I* did."

Epilogue

Reese
One year and eight months later

Oh my God. With my heart in my throat, I watch Brodie zoom down the ice, the stick in his hands moving so quickly back and forth that it seems like a blur. But he never once lets go of the puck and doesn't give the men gathering around him a chance to take it away. When he is almost to the goal, I glance up at the clock. He has seconds, and if he doesn't make this shot, his team is out of the running for the Cup. I don't want to watch, but I can't take my eyes off him.

When he swings his stick back, and it cracks against the ice, the sound ricocheting around the room. I stand up and swear time slows as the puck shoots past the men trying to catch it and goes into the goal.

"Holy shit!" I scream at the top of my lungs, my voice drowned out by the crowd cheering and the buzzer going off. He did it. I turn to one of the other player's wives, jumping up and down next to me, and the two of us embrace.

When she lets me go, I turn back to the rink and move closer to the glass with tears in my eyes. I will never admit it to anyone, especially not Brodie, because he would love to give me a hard time about it, but I love hockey. Or I love him, and he loves hockey so much that it's rubbed off on me. I laugh when I see him coming in my direction with his helmet off and a beautiful smile on his handsome face.

"You did it!" I scream at the top of my lungs. He rests his forehead against the glass, and I do the same, wishing I could touch him.

"Love you," he mouths when I lean back to look at him. I mouth it right back, then giggle when his teammates all swarm around him. Then, just like that, he's gone and out of sight, lost in the crowd of his friends.

Falling to my bottom in my seat, I let out a breath and then look at the screen when Aunt Ileana nudges me and points up. I frown when I realize that I'm looking at myself with the team's mascot right behind me. I turn around, and he holds out a tiny red box on his big furry paw.

"What?" I shake my head, and he motions for me to take it while the stadium buzzes around us. When I have it in my grasp, he hand-signals for me to open it, making me laugh. Lifting the lid on the box, my body stills, and my heart pounds.

The brightest and biggest diamond I have ever seen in my life glitters from inside, nestled in white silk. I look up at the mascot, confused.

"Turn around," people yell. When I do, I find Brodie still dressed in his hockey uniform, down on one knee behind me.

"Oh my God." I cover my mouth with my hand, and he reaches toward me and carefully takes the box from my grasp.

"Ree."

"No," I breathe, shaking my head. He laughs.

"I love you."

"Brodie." Tears fill my eyes.

"The last almost two years have been the happiest of my life." Oh, my God. My knees shake as I look into his eyes. "You're my best friend. The best thing to ever happen to me." I wipe the tears from my cheeks. "I know with you by my side, there is nothing I can't accomplish... Will you marry me?"

"Yes." I lunge at him and wrap my arms around his neck. The ground beneath my feet shakes as people scream, clap, and cheer. "I can't believe you," I whisper in his ear.

"I meant it. You're the best thing that's ever happened to me, Ree." I can't tell him that I feel the same because a sob I can't control is climbing up the back of my throat. I never imagined having a moment like this with a man as perfect for me as he is. "You said yes, right?" he asks against my ear, and I nod, then lean back to look at him while laughing.

"Yes." I wipe the tears from under my eyes as he takes my hand to slide the ring onto my finger. Once it's in place, he lifts my hand in the air, causing the crowd to go crazy again.

I laugh, leaning into him, then grab his face and give him a kiss that is likely too inappropriate for TV.

Brodie

Around 8 years later...

"Dada. Baba," my one-year-old daughter Rin shrieks. The people seated around us look in our direction, all with smiles on their faces directed at my girl, who looks just like her mom.

"Okay." I unclip her pacifier from her diaper bag and give it to her. As soon as she has it in her mouth, her head falls against my chest, and her eyes start to close. She's tired. Then again, she's had a busy few days, spending time with her older cousins and her grandparents, who are all in town for her mom's graduation.

Just when she starts to fall asleep, the president of the college calls Ree's name, and she steps onto the stage. Looking as beautiful as the day I met her, she walks up to the podium. The moment her voice comes through the speakers around the room, Rin sits up.

"She's right there." I point to where Ree is on the stage, and Rin's face lights up.

"Mama." Even from a distance, Ree hears Rin's voice and looks our way, smiling. But she doesn't falter in her valedictorian speech. I'm not surprised. My wife never falters. She also doesn't do anything half-assed. From being the best wife to the biggest cheerleader for me while I was still playing hockey and coming to every game she could—even when she claimed to hate sports. To being the most amazing mom to our daughter, all the while completing school. And not just completing it but *crushing* it and coming out at the top of her class. And even while doing all that, she still somehow found the time to make me fall a little more in love with her every single day.

And I know that will never change.

* * * *

Also from 1001 Dark Nights and Aurora Rose Reynolds, discover Keeping You.

Sign up for the 1001 Dark Nights Newsletter
and be entered to win a Tiffany Key necklace.

There's a contest every month!

Go to www.1001DarkNights.com to subscribe.

**As a bonus, all subscribers can download
FIVE FREE exclusive books!**

Discover 1001 Dark Nights Collection Eleven

DRAGON KISS by Donna Grant
A Dragon Kings Novella

THE WILD CARD by Dylan Allen
A Rivers Wilde Novella

ROCK CHICK REMATCH by Kristen Ashley
A Rock Chick Novella

JUST ONE SUMMER by Carly Phillips
A Dirty Dare Series Novella

HAPPILY EVER MAYBE by Carrie Ann Ryan
A Montgomery Ink Legacy Novella

BLUE MOON by Skye Warren
A Cirque des Moroirs Novella

A VAMPIRE'S MATE by Rebecca Zanetti
A Dark Protectors/Rebels Novella

LOVE HAZARD by Rachel Van Dyken

BRODIE by Aurora Rose Reynolds
An Until Her Novella

THE BODYGUARD AND THE BOMBSHELL by Lexi Blake
A Masters and Mercenaries: New Recruits Novella

THE SUBSTITUTE by Kristen Proby
A Single in Seattle Novella

CRAVED BY YOU by J. Kenner
A Stark Security Novella

GRAVEYARD DOG by Darynda Jones
A Charley Davidson Novella

A CHRISTMAS AUCTION by Audrey Carlan
A Marriage Auction Novella

THE GHOST OF A CHANCE by Heather Graham
A Krewe of Hunters Novella

Also from Blue Box Press

LEGACY OF TEMPTATION by Larissa Ione
A Demonica Birthright Novel

VISIONS OF FLESH AND BLOOD by Jennifer L. Armentrout and Ravyn Salvador
A Blood & Ash and Fire & Flesh Compendium

FORGETTING TO REMEMBER by M.J. Rose

TOUCH ME by J. Kenner
A Stark International Novella

BORN OF BLOOD AND ASH by Jennifer L. Armentrout
A Flesh and Fire Novel

MY ROYAL SHOWMANCE by Lexi Blake
A Park Avenue Promise Novel

SAPPHIRE DAWN by Christopher Rice writing as C. Travis Rice
A Sapphire Cove Novel

IN THE AIR TONIGHT by Marie Force

EMBRACING THE CHANGE by Kristen Ashley
A River Rain Novel

About Aurora Rose Reynolds

Aurora Rose Reynolds is a *New York Times*, *USA Today* and *Wall Street Journal* bestselling author whose wildly popular series include Until, Until Him, Until Her, Underground King, Shooting Stars, Fluke My Life and How to Catch an Alpha series.

Her writing career started in an attempt to get the outrageously alpha men who resided in her head to leave her alone and has blossomed into an opportunity to share her stories with readers all over the world.

Discover More Aurora Rose Reynolds

Keeping You: An Until Him/Her Novella

Having been put through the ringer by her ex who was a perpetual cheater and master manipulator, Bridgett doesn't have much faith in men. Then Noah comes into her life, a guy unlike any man she's ever known. Not only is he dependable, kind, and honest, he's too hot for his own good.

Not that any of that matters since Bridgett is still technically married, and Noah has made it clear without words that he's not interested.

So what's the worst that could happen when there's a fire and he offers her a place to crash until she can get back on her feet?

Protecting those in need comes with his job as a police officer, so Noah's not surprised by his need to protect Bridgett. The feelings of possessiveness when it comes to her are not something he knows how to deal with.

Noah knows he should keep her at arm's length, but instead of putting distance between them he keeps finding ways to bring them closer together and he's not sure if she will ever be close enough.

Before We Fall
By Aurora Rose Reynolds
Now available!

Tucker Beckett and I *likely never would have met if our spouses weren't having an affair.*

Newly divorced with a young son to raise Tucker Beckett is the last man Miranda Owens should be itching to figure out, to make smile, and hear laugh. Still there is something about the detective with haunted blue eyes and a dirty mouth that draws her in from the moment they meet.

If only life were so simple.

As Tucker and Miranda begin to navigate their new relationship, Tucker is tasked with solving the murder of a young woman, while their ex's begin to play games in an attempt to split the two of them up.

Before they fall, these two will need to figure out if the only thing tying them together is the circumstances that brought them together in the first place or if it's something more.

Love isn't complicated but sometimes life is.

* * * *

Chapter 1: Miranda

I'm going to be sick.

Holding my balled-up hand against my stomach, I read the text that just popped up on Bowie's computer again and try to convince myself that I'm misunderstanding what I'm looking at.

It doesn't work. No matter how many times I reread the message, it still says the same thing.

What time do you think you'll be here? Tucker is working late, so we don't need to worry about him.

The simple question seems innocent enough, but the photo attached to the message of a beautiful woman with dark hair who's wearing a red lace nightie proves I haven't made the wrong assumption.

"Mommy!" Kingston shouts, making me jump, and I slam the laptop closed and watch my beautiful boy with his dark hair and brown eyes—both traits from his father—hop-skip from the living room and into the kitchen. "Can we go outside now?"

"Yeah." I slid off the stool I pulled out so I could look up a recipe for dinner tonight, not having a clue that doing so would change everything. "Let Mommy get on her shoes."

"Okay," he sings, following behind me to the front door.

"How about we walk down to the park?" I suggest, putting on his coat first. It takes me a few tries to get it zipped, because my hands are shaking so badly.

"Yes." His tiny arms shoot into the air, and I can't help the smile that curves my lips.

"All right, let's go." I open the door after I've got my shoes on, and he bounces out ahead of me, then waits for me to lock up before he reaches for my hand.

Holding onto him tightly, I move on autopilot down the sidewalk, past house after house, all of them similar to the one Bowie moved us into just weeks after we found out we were pregnant with Kingston. Our boy was a surprise gift from our honeymoon in Jamaica and a complete shock to me, because I had been on birth control at the time and was not planning on being a mom.

Or not at that moment in my life anyway.

At that time, I was working at a hair salon as a stylist with a goal of opening my own shop within the next couple of years, but getting pregnant changed that. For the first five months, I was so sick that I could hardly get out of bed, and for the last four, I was put on bed rest, because my doctors were concerned I would miscarry.

Bowie was great about everything and had no problem stepping up and taking care of us when I could no longer work. And after we had Kingston, we just decided I would stay home until he started preschool. And with Bowie's job as a police officer, he was able to take an extra shift here or there, so we never struggled.

Now, I wonder if it was too much, if the responsibility and stress of him being the sole provider for our family changed the way he felt about me, about us.

With my throat tight, I shove that thought away. I might not work outside the house, but being a stay-at-home mom is a twenty-four-hour, seven-day-a-week gig. I do not get time off. Heck, I can't even remember the last time I went to the bathroom on my own, let alone left the house by myself. And when Bowie does have a day off, I always make sure he never has to worry about Kingston or anything around the house.

Just last weekend, he went out of town with friends to go fishing.

Or maybe he didn't. Maybe he spent the weekend banging another woman while I was home with our son.

Did I miss the signs? How long has it been going on?

Things between us have been... well, if I'm honest, *not great*. But that happens, right? The ups and downs in relationships, the times where you feel completely disconnected from your spouse. I know I've been feeling like that for a long time—longer than I'd even like to admit. I just convinced myself that things would get better when Kingston got a little older and he didn't need me so much.

"Mommy, can I go on the slide?" Kingston asks, dragging me from my thoughts, and I look around, realizing we've already made it the five blocks to the park.

"Yeah, just be careful on the way down."

"I know," he groans like he's had sixteen years of me annoying him with my overprotectiveness and not just three.

I watch him run across the mulch that covers the ground to the jungle gym with a slide attached, then I take a seat on the bench. Taking my phone out of my pocket, I tap the screen and see a message from Bowie letting me know he's going to be late tonight and not to wait up for him.

Numb, I message him back a quick Okay, when all I really want to do is rage, to tell him I know he's a liar, to ask how he could do this to us. He knows that cheating is not something I would ever forgive, not after growing up the way I did. My childhood was filled with turmoil, heartache, and confusion, watching my mom being cheated on by my dad and her constantly taking him back, knowing he'd just do it again.

That is not the life I want for our son. I do not want him to think that kind of relationship is normal, because it's not. And I deserve better than a man who would do that to me.

"Mommy, come push me!" Kingston shouts, and I tuck away the pain I'm feeling and head across the mulch, forcing a smile for my baby.

I have a lot of thinking to do. I'm not the only one in this situation, the only one who will be affected. And with me so dependent on Bowie, it's going to take me some time to leave.

Discover 1001 Dark Nights

COLLECTION ONE
FOREVER WICKED by Shayla Black ~ CRIMSON TWILIGHT by Heather Graham ~ CAPTURED IN SURRENDER by Liliana Hart ~ SILENT BITE: A SCANGUARDS WEDDING by Tina Folsom ~ DUNGEON GAMES by Lexi Blake ~ AZAGOTH by Larissa Ione ~ NEED YOU NOW by Lisa Renee Jones ~ SHOW ME, BABY by Cherise Sinclair~ ROPED IN by Lorelei James ~ TEMPTED BY MIDNIGHT by Lara Adrian ~ THE FLAME by Christopher Rice ~ CARESS OF DARKNESS by Julie Kenner

COLLECTION TWO
WICKED WOLF by Carrie Ann Ryan ~ WHEN IRISH EYES ARE HAUNTING by Heather Graham ~ EASY WITH YOU by Kristen Proby ~ MASTER OF FREEDOM by Cherise Sinclair ~ CARESS OF PLEASURE by Julie Kenner ~ ADORED by Lexi Blake ~ HADES by Larissa Ione ~ RAVAGED by Elisabeth Naughton ~ DREAM OF YOU by Jennifer L. Armentrout ~ STRIPPED DOWN by Lorelei James ~ RAGE/KILLIAN by Alexandra Ivy/Laura Wright ~ DRAGON KING by Donna Grant ~ PURE WICKED by Shayla Black ~ HARD AS STEEL by Laura Kaye ~ STROKE OF MIDNIGHT by Lara Adrian ~ ALL HALLOWS EVE by Heather Graham ~ KISS THE FLAME by Christopher Rice~ DARING HER LOVE by Melissa Foster ~ TEASED by Rebecca Zanetti ~ THE PROMISE OF SURRENDER by Liliana Hart

COLLECTION THREE
HIDDEN INK by Carrie Ann Ryan ~ BLOOD ON THE BAYOU by Heather Graham ~ SEARCHING FOR MINE by Jennifer Probst ~ DANCE OF DESIRE by Christopher Rice ~ ROUGH RHYTHM by Tessa Bailey ~ DEVOTED by Lexi Blake ~ Z by Larissa Ione ~ FALLING UNDER YOU by Laurelin Paige ~ EASY FOR KEEPS by Kristen Proby ~ UNCHAINED by Elisabeth Naughton ~ HARD TO SERVE by Laura Kaye ~ DRAGON FEVER by Donna Grant ~ KAYDEN/SIMON by Alexandra Ivy/Laura Wright ~ STRUNG UP by Lorelei James ~ MIDNIGHT UNTAMED by Lara Adrian ~ TRICKED by Rebecca Zanetti ~ DIRTY WICKED by Shayla Black ~ THE ONLY ONE by Lauren Blakely ~ SWEET SURRENDER by Liliana Hart

COLLECTION FOUR
ROCK CHICK REAWAKENING by Kristen Ashley ~ ADORING INK by Carrie Ann Ryan ~ SWEET RIVALRY by K. Bromberg ~ SHADE'S LADY by Joanna Wylde ~ RAZR by Larissa Ione ~ ARRANGED by Lexi Blake ~ TANGLED by Rebecca Zanetti ~ HOLD ME by J. Kenner ~ SOMEHOW, SOME WAY by Jennifer Probst ~ TOO CLOSE TO CALL by Tessa Bailey ~ HUNTED by Elisabeth Naughton ~ EYES ON YOU by Laura Kaye ~ BLADE by Alexandra Ivy/Laura Wright ~ DRAGON BURN by Donna Grant ~ TRIPPED OUT by Lorelei James ~ STUD FINDER by Lauren Blakely ~ MIDNIGHT UNLEASHED by Lara Adrian ~ HALLOW BE THE HAUNT by Heather Graham ~ DIRTY FILTHY FIX by Laurelin Paige ~ THE BED MATE by Kendall Ryan ~ NIGHT GAMES by CD Reiss ~ NO RESERVATIONS by Kristen Proby ~ DAWN OF SURRENDER by Liliana Hart

COLLECTION FIVE
BLAZE ERUPTING by Rebecca Zanetti ~ ROUGH RIDE by Kristen Ashley ~ HAWKYN by Larissa Ione ~ RIDE DIRTY by Laura Kaye ~ ROME'S CHANCE by Joanna Wylde ~ THE MARRIAGE ARRANGEMENT by Jennifer Probst ~ SURRENDER by Elisabeth Naughton ~ INKED NIGHTS by Carrie Ann Ryan ~ ENVY by Rachel Van Dyken ~ PROTECTED by Lexi Blake ~ THE PRINCE by Jennifer L. Armentrout ~ PLEASE ME by J. Kenner ~ WOUND TIGHT by Lorelei James ~ STRONG by Kylie Scott ~ DRAGON NIGHT by Donna Grant ~ TEMPTING BROOKE by Kristen Proby ~ HAUNTED BE THE HOLIDAYS by Heather Graham ~ CONTROL by K. Bromberg ~ HUNKY HEARTBREAKER by Kendall Ryan ~ THE DARKEST CAPTIVE by Gena Showalter

COLLECTION SIX
DRAGON CLAIMED by Donna Grant ~ ASHES TO INK by Carrie Ann Ryan ~ ENSNARED by Elisabeth Naughton ~ EVERMORE by Corinne Michaels ~ VENGEANCE by Rebecca Zanetti ~ ELI'S TRIUMPH by Joanna Wylde ~ CIPHER by Larissa Ione ~ RESCUING MACIE by Susan Stoker ~ ENCHANTED by Lexi Blake ~ TAKE THE BRIDE by Carly Phillips ~ INDULGE ME by J. Kenner ~ THE KING by Jennifer L. Armentrout ~ QUIET MAN by Kristen Ashley ~ ABANDON by Rachel Van Dyken ~ THE OPEN DOOR by Laurelin

Paige ~ CLOSER by Kylie Scott ~ SOMETHING JUST LIKE THIS by Jennifer Probst ~ BLOOD NIGHT by Heather Graham ~ TWIST OF FATE by Jill Shalvis ~ MORE THAN PLEASURE YOU by Shayla Black ~ WONDER WITH ME by Kristen Proby ~ THE DARKEST ASSASSIN by Gena Showalter

COLLECTION SEVEN
THE BISHOP by Skye Warren ~ TAKEN WITH YOU by Carrie Ann Ryan ~ DRAGON LOST by Donna Grant ~ SEXY LOVE by Carly Phillips ~ PROVOKE by Rachel Van Dyken ~ RAFE by Sawyer Bennett ~ THE NAUGHTY PRINCESS by Claire Contreras ~ THE GRAVEYARD SHIFT by Darynda Jones ~ CHARMED by Lexi Blake ~ SACRIFICE OF DARKNESS by Alexandra Ivy ~ THE QUEEN by Jen Armentrout ~ BEGIN AGAIN by Jennifer Probst ~ VIXEN by Rebecca Zanetti ~ SLASH by Laurelin Paige ~ THE DEAD HEAT OF SUMMER by Heather Graham ~ WILD FIRE by Kristen Ashley ~ MORE THAN PROTECT YOU by Shayla Black ~ LOVE SONG by Kylie Scott ~ CHERISH ME by J. Kenner ~ SHINE WITH ME by Kristen Proby

COLLECTION EIGHT
DRAGON REVEALED by Donna Grant ~ CAPTURED IN INK by Carrie Ann Ryan ~ SECURING JANE by Susan Stoker ~ WILD WIND by Kristen Ashley ~ DARE TO TEASE by Carly Phillips ~ VAMPIRE by Rebecca Zanetti ~ MAFIA KING by Rachel Van Dyken ~ THE GRAVEDIGGER'S SON by Darynda Jones ~ FINALE by Skye Warren ~ MEMORIES OF YOU by J. Kenner ~ SLAYED BY DARKNESS by Alexandra Ivy ~ TREASURED by Lexi Blake ~ THE DAREDEVIL by Dylan Allen ~ BOND OF DESTINY by Larissa Ione ~ MORE THAN POSSESS YOU by Shayla Black ~ HAUNTED HOUSE by Heather Graham ~ MAN FOR ME by Laurelin Paige ~ THE RHYTHM METHOD by Kylie Scott ~ JONAH BENNETT by Tijan ~ CHANGE WITH ME by Kristen Proby ~ THE DARKEST DESTINY by Gena Showalter

COLLECTION NINE
DRAGON UNBOUND by Donna Grant ~ NOTHING BUT INK by Carrie Ann Ryan ~ THE MASTERMIND by Dylan Allen ~ JUST ONE WISH by Carly Phillips ~ BEHIND CLOSED DOORS by Skye Warren ~ GOSSAMER IN THE DARKNESS by Kristen Ashley ~ THE

CLOSE-UP by Kennedy Ryan ~ DELIGHTED by Lexi Blake ~ THE GRAVESIDE BAR AND GRILL by Darynda Jones ~ THE ANTI-FAN AND THE IDOL by Rachel Van Dyken ~ CHARMED BY YOU by J. Kenner ~ DESCEND TO DARKNESS by Heather Graham~ BOND OF PASSION by Larissa Ione ~ JUST WHAT I NEEDED by Kylie Scott

COLLECTION TEN
DRAGON LOVER by Donna Grant ~ KEEPING YOU by Aurora Rose Reynolds ~ HAPPILY EVER NEVER by Carrie Ann Ryan ~ DESTINED FOR ME by Corinne Michaels ~ MADAM ALANA by Audrey Carlan ~ DIRTY FILTHY BILLIONAIRE by Laurelin Paige ~ TANGLED WITH YOU by J. Kenner ~ TEMPTED by Lexi Blake ~THE DANDELION DIARY by Devney Perry ~ CHERRY LANE by Kristen Proby ~ THE GRAVE ROBBER by Darynda Jones ~ CRY OF THE BANSHEE by Heather Graham ~ DARKEST NEED by Rachel Van Dyken ~ CHRISTMAS IN CAPE MAY by Jennifer Probst ~ A VAMPIRE'S MATE by Rebecca Zanetti ~ WHERE IT BEGINS by Helena Hunting

Discover Blue Box Press
TAME ME by J. Kenner ~ TEMPT ME by J. Kenner ~ DAMIEN by J. Kenner ~ TEASE ME by J. Kenner ~ REAPER by Larissa Ione ~ THE SURRENDER GATE by Christopher Rice ~ SERVICING THE TARGET by Cherise Sinclair ~ THE LAKE OF LEARNING by Steve Berry and M.J. Rose ~ THE MUSEUM OF MYSTERIES by Steve Berry and M.J. Rose ~ TEASE ME by J. Kenner ~ FROM BLOOD AND ASH by Jennifer L. Armentrout ~ QUEEN MOVE by Kennedy Ryan ~ THE HOUSE OF LONG AGO by Steve Berry and M.J. Rose ~ THE BUTTERFLY ROOM by Lucinda Riley ~ A KINGDOM OF FLESH AND FIRE by Jennifer L. Armentrout ~ THE LAST TIARA by M.J. Rose ~ THE CROWN OF GILDED BONES by Jennifer L. Armentrout ~ THE MISSING SISTER by Lucinda Riley ~ THE END OF FOREVER by Steve Berry and M.J. Rose ~ THE STEAL by C. W. Gortner and M.J. Rose ~ CHASING SERENITY by Kristen Ashley ~ A SHADOW IN THE EMBER by Jennifer L. Armentrout ~ THE BAIT by C.W. Gortner and M.J. Rose ~ THE FASHION ORPHANS by Randy Susan Meyers and M.J. Rose ~ TAKING THE LEAP by Kristen Ashley ~ SAPPHIRE SUNSET by Christopher Rice writing C. Travis Rice ~ THE WAR OF TWO QUEENS by Jennifer L. Armentrout ~ THE

MURDERS AT FLEAT HOUSE by Lucinda Riley ~ THE HEIST by C.W. Gortner and M.J. Rose ~ SAPPHIRE SPRING by Christopher Rice writing as C. Travis Rice ~ MAKING THE MATCH by Kristen Ashley ~ A LIGHT IN THE FLAME by Jennifer L. ~ THE MARRIAGE AUCTION by Audrey Carlan ~ THE JEWELER OF STOLEN DREAMS by M.J. Rose ~ SAPPHIRE STORM by Christopher Rice writing as C. Travis Rice ~ ATLAS: THE STORY OF PA SALT by Lucinda Riley and Harry Whittaker ~ LOVE ON THE BYLINE by Xio Axelrod ~ A SOUL OF ASH AND BLOOD by Jennifer L. Armentrout ~ START US UP by Lexi Blake ~ FIGHTING THE PULL by Kristen Ashley ~ A FIRE IN THE FLESH by Jennifer L. Armentrout

On Behalf of 1001 Dark Nights,
Liz Berry, M.J. Rose, and Jillian Stein would like to thank ~

Steve Berry
Doug Scofield
Benjamin Stein
Kim Guidroz
Chelle Olson
Tanaka Kangara
Asha Hossain
Chris Graham
Jessica Saunders
Stacey Tardif
Dylan Stockton
Kate Boggs
Richard Blake
and Simon Lipskar

Made in the USA
Columbia, SC
01 July 2024